Outpost of Jupiter

Outpost of Jupiter

Lester del Rey

Holt, Rinehart and Winston
New York / Chicago / San Francisco

*To Carol Webb, who taught the sciences
and practised the humanities.*

Contents

The Frozen Worlds

SOMEDAY, long after Mars has been explored and perhaps colonized, men are going to want to go farther out into space, to the huge planet Jupiter, to ringed Saturn, and eventually even to the distant challenge of Pluto. Such exploration will have to wait for much better rockets than we now have, or for completely different space ships. But when the power to go is developed, the ships will be sent hurtling outwards to where Jupiter circles nearly five hundred million miles from the Sun. Maybe some of those who go outwards will never return, but will find new homes and new ways of life on the distant worlds. It seems impossible now, but sometimes the impossible only takes a little longer to come true.

No man is ever going to live on Jupiter, however. That giant planet, eleven times the diameter of Earth, is totally unfit for human life. Gravity there would make an average man weigh over 400 pounds and no rocket imaginable would be powerful enough to permit landing and taking off again. There may not even be a crust on which to land, since some theories indicate that the tremendously compressed atmosphere 600 miles down may simply blend with frozen solids, leaving no true surface. The pressure there is ten times greater than at the deepest part of Earth's oceans, and the temperature is about 20° below zero Fahrenheit. There is no oxygen to breathe; the atmosphere seems to be composed of methane, a gas used as a fuel on Earth, with clouds of frozen ammonia crystals. It would be easier to explore planets around other stars than to exist on Jupiter.

Fortunately, Jupiter has a system of moons, like ready-made space stations, from which the giant primary can be studied. Eight are quite small, but the other four are nearly of planetary size. These four were discovered by Galileo in 1610, and are named Io, Europa, Ganymede, and Callisto, after mythological human associates of the Roman god Jupiter. Io and Europa are about the size of Earth's Moon. Farther out, Ganymede and Callisto are nearly as large as Mars. Either of these would make a good base from which to observe Jupiter.

Callisto offers its own mysteries, too. In spite of its size, it is little more than half as heavy as our Moon, which means it must either be made of something lighter than ice or else must not be solid; either possibility is equally mystifying. But Callisto would hardly do for long-range use, since a man would weigh only seven or eight pounds there—too light for comfortable working and living conditions.

None of the moons seem suitable for colonizing. All are airless, which would make life impossible outside a spacesuit or a completely enclosed colony. All are frigidly cold, probably colder even than Jupiter, since they have no atmospheres to retain what little heat does reach them from the distant Sun.

Ganymede is probably the most promising of the four major moons. It is the largest, 3,300 miles in diameter, with a surface gravity similar to that of Earth's Moon. It circles Jupiter once in a little more than a week, at a distance of 650,000 miles, apparently turning the same face toward the primary at all times. In doing so, it rotates under the light from the Sun, to yield day and night periods of about 86 hours each. With the huge globe of Jupiter reflecting the sunlight at night, however, the difference between night and day must be slight.

Yet this frozen, airless world offers almost nothing, so far as we know, to encourage men to live there. So why should men want to set up a colony on such a forbidding place?

Nobody can answer that question today. But why should men have chosen to live in the frozen North on Earth when life is so much easier in other lands? We can only guess that men will find reasons when they get there, as they have found reasons to live wherever they have gone in the past.

One reason might be the discovery of plant life on Ganymede which might yield new drugs or other products that would pay for the tremendous shipping costs back to Earth. From what we know now, this seems almost impossible. No plants that we know could exist on the frozen little world. Yet life is a strange phenomenon, finding ways to exist where conditions are apparently hopeless. Plants grow in the ice of the Arctic and in the nearly boiling water of some hot springs. Primitive one-celled life exists deep in our oil wells, living without air. Many scientists believe there are plants on Mars, and others report that there is evidence for some kind of life on the Moon. We are just beginning to explore the secrets of life today, and we cannot make any accurate guesses as to what is possible. From what we know, living cells cannot possibly move or divide to form others under the pressure found in some ocean trenches, yet those trenches are filled with busy, multiplying forms of life. We have no idea how such life survives, nor can we know yet whether life could adapt to conditions on Ganymede.

The exploration of space will be made one step at a time. Before our ships reach out to the worlds around Jupiter, there will be colonies on the Moon and Mars. The experience gained in mastering such inhospitable worlds will make it much easier to overcome the difficulties found on Ganymede. Then the colonies near Jupiter will be steps to further progress. Saturn, of course, is unsuitable for human life, since conditions would be similar to those on Jupiter; but the great rings around the planet will need closer exploration, and Saturn has a large moon, named Titan, on which a base can be established. From there we may go on to still further planets and eventually, perhaps, to the stars.

The farther we go, the more difficult it becomes to imagine what the future will be like. There are limits to our ability to guess what may develop from man's leap into space.

To me, however, it seems safe to assume that men will not only reach the moons of Jupiter but will establish an outpost colony on at least one of them. So long as there are frontiers of space or of the mind, there will be frontiersmen to explore them.

—L. DEL R.

1 / Danger Signal

FAR OUT IN SPACE, the greatest ship ever built by men went hurtling inward from Titan toward Ganymede at nearly a million miles an hour. That speed had been built up two weeks before, during the first twelve hours after take-off from Saturn's moon. Now the *Procyon* coasted effortlessly on its momentum. The huge drive motors that filled most of the interior were still. The ship should have been almost as silent as the void through which it sped.

There was no silence outside the little cabin Bob Wilson shared with his father, however. As he dressed, feet pounded up and down the hallway and there were shouts that he couldn't quite understand. Then there was a sharp knock on his door.

"Bob! You're wanted in Control in ten minutes!"

He glanced at his father, but Dr. Wilson seemed to be asleep still. Bob slipped the door aside as quietly as he could and stepped out into the hallway, where Red Mullins was waiting for him.

Red was eighteen—the same age as Bob; but there all resemblance ceased. Bob was tall, thin, and dark, while Red was under average height, solidly built, with round features and a flaming red crew cut that had given him his nickname.

From the rear of the hallway, there was a sudden yell and the crash of metal. A crew technician came running forward, shouting back something about a larger lock wrench.

"What goes on?" Bob asked. "And why would they want me in Control?"

Red shrugged. "They didn't say. Just told me to get you up. And nobody seems to know what happened, except that we got hit! I thought it must have been the danger gong that waked you."

"Maybe it was," Bob agreed. He could dimly remember some unusual sound that had cut through his sleep. All the stories he'd read of ships being hit by meteoroids in space came back to him, and he felt himself tensing. But the air was still circulating normally, and there was no danger signal now. Anyhow, the *Procyon* was supposed to be almost invulnerable. "How do I get to Control?"

"I'll take you. They're yelling for coffee up there." Red served as steward and ship's messenger during his duty shift. Now he turned back to the galley.

Bob followed him. Then he began helping while Red gathered up two trays and began loading them. He took the smaller tray as they headed forward, with Red leading the way through the maze of little hallways. The *Procyon* had been designed around the great drive motors, since those had to be huge to work at all. They climbed twisting stairs around the motors, took other hallways, and finally began climbing again.

"Want to rest?" Red asked. "We can take a minute."

Bob shook his head. His legs were tired, but he knew Red would never have thought of resting for his own comfort. Bob had discovered to his surprise that the other was stronger than he was, and in better condition. "Where did you grow muscles, Red? I thought a man weighed only about twenty-five pounds on Ganymede."

"That's right. So you Earthmen think we're all weaklings," Red smiled slowly. "Doesn't work that way. Inertia is still the same. Anyhow, most of the time I wore a vacuum suit—a real working suit, not one of these light emergency things they use on ships. With all the equipment on that, I carry more weight at home than I do on Earth."

They had reached the end of the hallway now and were entering the control section of the ship. Bob had never been there before, and he was surprised at the size. A large room served as chart room and captain's bridge. It was filled with tables and desks, and on the walls were huge viewing screens that looked like windows into space. The *Procyon* had no true ports, but picked up the scene on television cameras concealed in the hull. There were two smaller conning rooms located off the main one, each filled with other screens, panels of instruments, and calculators. Andrews, the navigator, was busy in one of those, while Captain Rokoff and Chief Engineer Haikato were in the main room, arguing over a big schematic with the other officers.

Anderson spotted Bob and motioned for the boy to join him. "I hear you can use a calculator, Wilson. How good are you? Can you handle tensor and vector analysis? Or simple harmonic functions?"

"Maybe." Bob couldn't accept any functions as simple.

He had been coached by his father in mathematics, and had taken all the courses he could on computer programming, since that would be necessary when he specialized in analytic linguistics. "Mostly, I've studied statistical analysis, though I've had a lot of calculus."

Andrews sighed, and then grinned. "Oh. Well, I guess you'll do. I've worked out the rough steps, and about all you have to do is feed the information into the machine. You'll save me a lot of time, and that may be important. Okay?"

"I'll try," Bob agreed. "What happened, Mr. Andrews? Are we in serious trouble?"

"Who knows? Something hit us. Now either our instruments are wrong or we've lost the protective field over one rear section." Andrews shrugged. "At our speed and without the field another hit would be a lot worse than serious. It would be fatal!"

Bob shivered as he took the notes and went into the other cabin to use the computer there. His eyes went to the viewing screens. Space seemed empty, except for the distant sun and stars, but Bob knew that a meteoroid far too small to register on the screen was more than enough to wreck them completely.

The explosive energy of a collision was proportional to the masses of the objects and to the square of the speed! A small bit of matter striking a normal low-speed ship might be traveling only twenty miles a second and still wreck the ship. The *Procyon*'s speed of nearly three hundred miles a second would produce at least two hundred times as much explosive fury. And space was never completely empty.

Bob couldn't fully understand the protective field,

16

which seemed to be related both to gravity and magnetism. He knew only that it acted in one direction, and was adjusted to push outward from the skin of the ship. Anything in the path of the *Procyon* was deflected by the field until it swung out of the ship's path. Without such protection, the use of high-speed spaceships was impossible.

An adaptation of the field was built into the ceilings to give a downward thrust to everything below so as to simulate normal gravity while the ship coasted. Other ships were weightless, once the drive ceased, but aboard the *Procyon* the apparent weight could be adjusted to Earth normal. Still another adaptation drove the ship itself, though that involved theories of physics that were far beyond anything Bob could grasp.

The computer began clucking quietly as he fed it the data Andrews had given him. One of the larger machines could have done everything itself from the breakdown of procedure in the notes, but this one had a limited capacity—it was only slightly better than the one Bob had in his cabin. He had to stop periodically and feed back former results, but it was routine enough for him to be sure he was making no mistakes.

Part of the time he was able to listen to the conversation of Captain Rokoff, but he couldn't make too much sense out of it, since most of it related to technicalities about the ship. But he could sense the tension mounting as the reports came in.

Andrews must have heard Bob's grunt of relief as the last bit of information came from the computer. He came in and picked up the results at once. Rokoff joined him, and they went back to the other cabin, where Andrews fed the combination of Bob's work and his own into the other computer.

"Drat!" The navigator ripped the typed results out in disgust. "Two traces! What the radar spotted and what the hull indicators picked up were not the same object."

"You mean you can't find the center of the hit?" Rokoff asked.

Andrews shook his head, frowning over the mathematics. "Worse than that! According to this, there was no center —whatever hit was spread over the whole section. It looks as if we'd been hit by another field instead of by a solid object."

"But that's impossible. We're the only ship operating with the field. The *Centaurus* won't be launched for three more years." Rokoff bent over the equations, then nodded reluctantly. "You're right, though. And that's what the tests we've been running indicate, too. It means we'll have to run checks over the whole hull section. Four hours, at least!"

He dashed back into the main room, shouting orders as he went. The men and officers began filing out quickly, with the Captain following them.

Andrews moved into the control seat, staring at the screens. "Nothing I can do, but someone has to watch, I guess," he told Bob. "If anything is coming for that section, it will hit before we can correct our course."

"Anything else I can do?" Bob asked.

"No. You did a good job, but that's all over now." Andrews smiled briefly. "Thanks. You can stick around, if you like. Just keep out of the way, and nobody will mind."

Bob went back into the main room where he could

watch the big screen that showed the rear section of the hull. Andrews had guessed correctly that he hated to go back to his own cabin and not know what was going on. But there was very little to see. From time to time, some of the ship's officers came back to study the diagrams or issue orders, but mostly he was alone there.

Red Mullins came in half an hour later. His duty shift must have been over, since he'd taken off his brief jacket, but he seemed to have the freedom of the ship. "Some of the scientific staff are awake," he reported to Andrews. "I told them we'd taken a small hit and were making repairs. Hi, Bob. I told your father you were up here watching."

The scientific staff were mostly biologists and biochemists, who would be of little use in repairing the ship. They had been recruited after the *Procyon* came back from the first voyage to Saturn with news that there might be life on Titan. Bob's father had insisted on taking Bob, since the boy had no mother or other relatives; and because Dr. Wilson was probably Earth's leading biochemist specializing on alien life, permission had been granted. Now, after three months, they were returning with the primitive plants they had collected, eager to begin analyzing what they had discovered. Bob was equally anxious to get back to college before too much of the semester was over.

From the navigation panel there was the sudden sound of a buzzer. Bob jerked his head around to see red lights glaring and something bright on one of the screens. Then it was gone, and the buzzer was silent.

Andrews laughed shakily. "False alarm. That one just missed us," he called to the boys. "I've got the screen sensitivity stretched to the limit, or nothing would have registered."

Bob settled slowly back to his seat. There was an ache in the small of his back where his adrenal glands must have sprung into frightened activity, and his hands were unsteady. Red's face was also strained as the other boy dropped to a nearby chair.

"Right now I'd even be happy to find myself back on Earth," he said.

Bob tried to take his eyes off the screen. Sitting and staring in silence was the worst thing he could do. "What brought you to Earth before, if you don't like it there?" he asked.

"School," Red answered. "Dad wanted me to take some special courses, so he arranged to transfer to Earth for two years to do government research in return for my tuition. He was a top-flight chemical engineer."

"Where is he now? Back on Ganymede?"

Red's face tautened, and he sighed. "He and Mom were asleep in their apartment when the *Helvetia* crashed on the building. I was at school," he said quietly. "Now I'm going back to live with my uncle."

"I'm sorry." Bob had read of the tragic crash of the *Helvetia*, returning from the Moon. There had been hints of scandal, and the government had been quietly settling claims ever since. Red must have been entitled to almost anything he chose to ask for. "So that's why you were allowed to ship back on the *Procyon?*"

Before Red could answer, Andrews broke in. "Red wasn't allowed, Wilson—he was asked! They needed someone to take the scientists around—someone who knew how to find life on a frozen, impossible moon, and Ganymede's more like Titan than any other place we know. He volunteered, just as he volunteered to act as steward, though he's technically part of the science staff. Didn't your father tell you that?"

Bob shook his head. Maybe Dr. Wilson had told him, but he hadn't listened. He'd still been full of Earth snobbery on the trip out, unwilling to associate with colonials or crewmen. On Titan, he'd deeply resented the fact that Red was permitted to go out with the scientists, while he was largely confined to the ship. It wasn't until the return trip that he'd begun to realize he couldn't help liking the other boy. Now he felt himself flushing in embarrassment as he remembered that he had been allowed to come only as a favor to his father. Maybe Red should have been the one who looked down on him!

"Forget it," Red said to Andrews. "Bob's all right." He turned his glance back toward the screen that showed the rear of the ship. "There's a bubble attached to that section of the hull. Can you tell which one it is, Mr. Andrews?"

Andrews adjusted a small control dial, and the view on the screen changed, to show the bubble. It was a pointed half-cylinder of metal attached to the main hull. There were half a dozen of these, and they served as storage holds for supplies and tools. They had been attached to the *Procyon* for the expedition to Titan, since the normal storage space had proved inadequate for the needs of the large science staff.

"Bubble C," Red muttered unhappily as Andrews brought the bubble into focus. The navigator began moving the dial back to its former position, but Red still stared gloomily at the screen. "It would be. That's the bubble containing all the supplies we are supposed to deliver to Ganymede. If anything happens to that, it means hard times for the colony."

Rokoff came dashing in before Bob could try to express sympathy. The Captain's suit was smeared with grease, and the two crewmen with him were even dirtier. He headed for a large cabinet against one wall and began drawing out what looked like wiring diagrams, sorting them hastily and handing three to the men. They went dashing out again at once.

"The field coils in the whole section are burned out," Rokoff told Andrews. "Looks like an overload. It will take us at least two hours to replace them, if we're lucky." He found a bunch of keys and tossed them to Red. "Take those down to Haikato, will you? And you might put out a general call to the passengers, Andrews. Just that the trouble has been found and is being repaired."

He went back again, leaving Andrews and Bob alone in the control section. Bob had always thought of the Captain as staying on the bridge, issuing terse orders but not really working. Apparently in this emergency, Rokoff was more needed to supervise the actual work.

"Why are we carrying supplies to Ganymede, Mr. Andrews?" he asked when the navigator had finished at the intercom. "I thought we were just dropping Red there. This isn't exactly a cargo ship."

Andrews frowned in surprise. "Interspace charters. Any ship passing near any colony has to carry supplies by charter rules, just as the colonies have to keep a space tug and repair facilities for the ships. We have to pass near Jupiter on the return flight, so we carry freight. Weren't you ever interested in space? I thought all boys on Earth were spacehappy enough to know all about it."

Bob shook his head. He'd started helping his father with the computer needed for biochemical analysis years before and had become so interested in the problem of communication between men and machine that he hadn't had time for space. It still didn't interest him much, though most of his friends were space fans.

Time dragged. Twice he started to leave the control section, but the screens still held him. If anything did strike, it would be over so quickly that he could hardly see it, but he found it impossible not to watch.

Andrews got up for coffee and reached for a cigarette, to find the pack empty. He tossed it away and stepped out into the hallway toward the lockers there. For a moment, he was out of sight.

Abruptly, the buzzer cut in, followed at once by the hammering of a gong. Danger signal! The board was lighting up, but Bob caught only a glimpse of it as he jerked his head around to the screen showing the rear of the ship.

2 / Attack from Nowhere

BOB'S FIRST SHOCKED REACTION was that it was already over. There was an object on the screen, but it was already far behind the ship. Then he saw that the object was drawing nearer. The attack was coming from the rear!

Out in space, behind the *Procyon* was a strange globe of white. As it rushed up, it seemed to be about three hundred feet in diameter, with no features on the outside. It came straight toward the damaged hull section, seemed to touch, and then veered off.

There was a shock that rang through the *Procyon*. Somewhere from the rear, metal screamed, and the deck under Bob's feet trembled. Now gongs were sounding everywhere. But Bob kept his eyes on the screen. The huge globe was lifting away, ripping part of the hull of the *Procyon* with it. And suddenly the screen went blank.

Andrews had been thrown into the locker. Now he wrenched himself free and dashed for the controls. He cut off the gongs with a flip of a switch while his other hand opened the intercom switch.

"Suits!" he shouted. "We're losing air."

There was a clang and thump from the rear. Automatic seals were slamming into place, cutting off the section from which air was leaking. Andrews had started to drag out a light suit from an emergency locker, but now he slipped it back. He caught sight of Bob and motioned out toward the hall.

"Get back to your father!" he ordered. "And if anyone asks you, tell them the ship is still sound."

Bob ran down the hallway, noticing that the suit lockers had opened automatically, to show suits hanging on their hooks. He had gone through suit drills, but he was glad he hadn't been forced to put one on in a hurry. Rokoff and the First Officer came down the hall as he reached the stairs. The Captain was wearing a suit, but the helmet was thrown back.

Somehow, Bob found his way through the maze of stairs and corridors. His feet seemed to retrace his path by themselves, since his mind was too full of what he'd seen to bother guiding him.

There couldn't be ships that could catch the *Procyon* from the rear! No other ship known had speed enough. Yet he'd seen the globe pull up effortlessly. And why should it deliberately attack? From where had it come?

He tried to throw off the burden of his worries as he reached the passenger lounge. Here most of the men had struggled into suits. He saw that one young biologist had managed to get a suit on backwards, but most had reacted properly to the signals that indicated loss of air. Now a few were beginning to remove the suits, though most seemed unwilling to give up the added safety.

The loud speaker was blaring over their heads in the

unmistakable voice of Captain Rokoff. "The emergency is over! The hull breach has been sealed, and there is no loss of air. Passengers will please remain in their own section while the crew attends to necessary work! I repeat, everything is under control. Please resume your breakfast."

It was penetrating through the aura of half-panic that had begun, and the little clumps of men were beginning to break up.

Bob found Red circulating among the staff, directing people to seats, where other stewards were serving coffee. "Your father is in your cabin," Red called.

Bob nodded his thanks, and headed there. He found his father sitting on the edge of the bunk, calmly tying his shoelaces. He should have guessed that Dr. Wilson wouldn't panic. His space suit had been neatly folded and hung back in the locker, and now the older man was calmly dressing for breakfast.

Dr. Wilson was fifty, but his hair and neat little goatee were still jet black. He looked tired still, Bob noticed, but less so than during the grueling labor of exploring Titan. Now he smiled at Bob. "Good morning, Bob. I hear from Red you've been having a busy time. Had breakfast?"

Bob realized suddenly that he hadn't eaten since waking. And with the thought, he found hunger sweeping over him. Five minutes before, he'd have sworn he couldn't even think of food, but now he was glad to find a table set for him and his father.

In the last few moments, the panic seemed to have evaporated completely from the section. Scientists could react to fear and danger as quickly and blindly as anyone else, but they had better control of their imaginations when assured the threat was gone.

Bob wondered how completely the danger was past. There had still been half an hour's work on restoring the protective field when the ship was hit, and there was no guessing how much damage had been done. But he kept quiet about his own doubts. Around him, the conversation was already beginning to resume its normal course, with most of the tables filled with the busy sounds of men eating.

Dr. Wang dropped into a chair beside Bob's father, setting down a tray loaded with food. The little man complained constantly about his loss of appetite with age, but he managed to eat enough for any three men. He smiled at Bob, then turned to Dr. Wilson.

"I finished my preliminary calculation on the former atmosphere of Titan," he announced. "And it indicates no possibility of life having been formed there by the usual amino acid method. Apparently that confirms the theory that all life in the Solar System must have originated on Earth and been carried into space by the splashing of Earth soil under the impact of meteorites."

Dr. Wilson nodded. "I thought that was amply proved by the proportion of the aminos in Ganymedan life. We've known for a century that a meteorite striking a planet can throw up material at a velocity high enough to carry it into space."

Bob could follow the conversation. He'd been following such conversations since he was able to talk. But he had very little of his father's interest in the puzzles of biology. He finished his breakfast and excused himself. Red was about finished serving, and Bob followed him out to the galley.

"Any more word?" he asked the young steward.

Red shrugged. "I took coffee to the men working on the section, but didn't learn much. They seemed to be about finished with repairs. They'd better be. We can't take another hit. We were lucky that this was a glancing one, I guess. Did you see what happened to the bubble?"

"Gone," Bob decided. He hadn't really seen, but he had a vague memory of the hull section just before the camera was wrecked. The globe had struck directly at the bubble. "I'm sorry, Red."

Red sighed. "I knew it, of course. The hull rupture was right below the bubble. It's going to make things tough without the uranium slugs and supplies they need back home, but maybe we'll get an emergency shipment. Darn it, every cent I got paid for this trip was in supplies there!"

"Doesn't insurance cover that?" Bob asked.

"Sure—eventually. But I wanted Uncle Frank to have his microscope when I got there. Did you see anything of the hit?"

Bob nodded slowly. "Yeah. I think so." He tried to describe what he'd seen, while Red stared at him doubtfully. There was an odd expression in the green eyes of the steward. "Are there any other stories of alien spacecraft?" Bob asked finally. "I mean, like the old flying saucer accounts we studied in school?"

"*You* studied, maybe," Red said. "Nobody on the outplanets takes such courses. I thought they'd found out all about the atmospheric disturbances that caused people to think they saw flying discs."

Bob knew the theory of electromagnetic disturbances, too. He was grasping at straws for an explanation. It seemed ridiculous that any alien ship from another star—if there were such ships—should attack senselessly; alien explorers would be looking for peace, not warfare. And if such a super-ship, capable of crossing light years of space, should strike, its technology should be advanced enough to wipe out its target without leaving a trace.

"You don't believe me, Red?" he asked when the other remained silent.

Red shrugged. "I don't know, Bob. I believe you saw something funny, but what it was or what it means is more than I like to guess. Come on, we'd better get back."

There was an announcement over the intercom as they reached the dining section. "All repairs have been success-fully completed. The *Procyon* is now completely space-worthy, and no further danger is anticipated. Damage was confined to a single supply bubble. The ship's routine will now resume until landing on Ganymede. This is Captain Rokoff. I want to thank you for remaining calm and for co-operating during the emergency, and to assure you that there is no further danger." The announcement ended. Then the voice of the signal officer came.

"Robert Wilson, please report to the Captain!"

Dr. Wilson glanced at his son. "Trouble, Bob?"

"No, sir. I'm not in trouble. I expect he just wants a re-port."

Wilson nodded. "Good. In that case, I'll come along if you don't mind."

He'd always believed in letting Bob face his own troubles with teachers or other boys, unless his son asked for help.

There was still some evidence of the past emergency. Crewmen were dragging supplies back to their proper place, and one of the hallways was a tangle of electric wiring. But everything looked normal in the control section. The schematics had been put away, the desks cleared, and Captain Rokoff had washed and changed into a clean uniform. He was taking reports over the intercom, but seemed satisfied with what he heard.

He nodded at Bob, then lifted his eyebrow as he saw the boy's father.

"I'll tell him anyway, unless you order me not to," Bob said. He preferred to have his father hear it at the same time as the Captain. The longer he waited, the harder it was to remember exactly what little he had seen.

Rokoff smiled. "Very good. I'm sure we can trust Dr. Wilson's discretion, if there's anything you have to report. Andrews suggested you may have seen something before we were hit, and I want your observations for my report."

Here in the sane world of the restored control section, Bob found it difficult to marshal his observations. At Rokoff's suggestion, he took a seat before the screen, exactly as he had been sitting when the hit occurred. He could see that the screen was working again and that there was a scar where the bubble had been, with plates roughly welded over the hull there. He began with his fleeting sight of the red lights over the control panel, and then his first impression of the globe.

"From behind?" Rokoff asked. "You're sure of that?"

"It looked that way." He went ahead, seeing doubt growing in the eyes of the Captain. Hearing the story from his own lips, he found it hard to believe himself. Even his father was frowning as he finished.

Rokoff sat back, staring down at the tape recorder that had been making a record of the story.

"Did you ever read any space pirate stories, Bob?" the Captain asked finally.

Dr. Wilson answered for him. "Not many, Captain. I'm afraid my son never accepted the romance of space. I'm the one who reads such tales."

"I read them myself when I get the chance," Rokoff said. He smiled. "You've got to admit this sounds exactly like something out of one of those stories, though. The strange ship, not like any we have. The sudden attack at greater speed —when we're already going ten times as fast as any other ship ever built. And the seizure of booty and the retreat. Maybe we're lucky not to have been boarded and scuttled, eh?" He shook his head. "The only trouble is that there are no pirates in space and never were—"

"So far as we know," Bob amended cautiously. He hadn't thought of piracy, but it was at least as good an explanation as that of a ship from beyond the Solar System.

Rokoff shook his head firmly. "No—we can be sure there are no pirates, Bob. Oh, I know there are reports of such raids. Every time a ship is lost or ruined by a meteoroid, the newspapers suggest foul play. But a space ship costs so much that only the government can afford to build one—and there have been no ships lost without being traced. Besides, any

31

man smart enough to design a ship capable of piracy would make far more money turning his plans over to the government than he could make from a life of crime."

"You mean you don't believe me?" Bob asked.

"I believe you," Rokoff assured him. "I think you have told me exactly what your eyes told you. But I wouldn't believe my own eyes in a situation like that. Can you be sure that the object came from behind? Look, if something hit the ship's field before striking that section, it would be heated. It would turn pretty bright and begin to vaporize, making it swell in size. Wouldn't that look like something coming from behind and growing nearer?"

Bob considered it. He'd been watching through a screen which showed no true depth and which would reproduce a blowing mass of hot gas as simply something white. "What about the fact that it hit later and that it then turned off sideways?"

"Probably it did hit later—you first saw it ahead of the section. And on hitting, it rebounded."

The explanation almost fitted the facts. Bob shrugged. He couldn't prove that the Captain was wrong without transferring his own mental image to the other—and language wasn't capable of such precise detail.

"I'm not trying to put you through the third degree," Rokoff went on. "Officially, and personally, I'm happy to get any direct observation. We'll need it in the records for later study. These protective fields are still too new to let anything like this pass without a full examination. But I have to look for the simplest explanation."

"It seems to me the fact that your field was breached

the first time is pretty fantastic by itself," Dr. Wilson suggested. "I thought nothing could get through."

Rokoff grimaced. "You're too right, Doctor. I'd almost rather believe some other ship came alongside just out of radar range with some mysterious ray and broke the field first, before attacking. It would make a lot tidier story. But it would also need the existence of a mysterious ship and some kind of radiation we know nothing about, and I can't buy such an idea yet. I'd rather put it down to the well-proven fact that men's eyes trick them. I saw a meteoroid once that looked exactly like a cow—but the film of it showed almost no resemblance. I filled in most of it in my own mind. Oh, I saw the cow, and in complete detail! But it was a trick of light and shadow."

He thanked Bob again and dismissed him. Dr. Wilson went along as they returned to the passenger lounge. The older man stared at his son. "I'm afraid I'm on the Captain's side in this, Bob," he decided. "I think you reported things exactly as you saw them but that your eyes tricked you. If that 'ship' you thought you saw turned as suddenly sideways as you said, what kind of acceleration pressure would the occupants have to stand?"

Bob hadn't thought of that. It was a good question. The answer was in hundreds of gravities of pressure—more than flesh could take. "Unless they had some kind of device to cancel inertia," he said doubtfully.

"You see? To accept your theory, one impossible assumption on top of another is needed. And you remember the rule of Occam's razor: 'Normally, that explanation is best which meets all objections with the simplest set of assumptions.' I don't think I'd talk much about it to others, if I were you."

Bob had already decided on that. If even his father thought he was unconsciously romanticizing, then anyone else would consider his wild story an outright fabrication.

Yet in his own mind he was sure that the simple explanation didn't fit in this case. He hadn't been prepared mentally to accept a spaceship out there, nor was he accustomed to fantasy. And the picture he remembered of the object coming in directly for a planned hit against the bubble, then veering off with it, was full of tiny details that he was sure hadn't simply been painted in by his mind. If he'd had a camera turned on and recording. . . . But he had only his own words to prove his case, and they were inadequate.

He talked it over with Red later, since he'd already told him the story. Surprisingly, Red seemed more doubtful of the Captain's explanation than he'd expected.

"I don't know, Bob. I've heard some strange stories before. If you think you saw a ship, I won't say you didn't, though I can't make myself really believe in it. I hope you didn't, though."

"Why?"

"Because if the field failed and we took a normal hit, I can feel fairly safe now that they've repaired things." Red grunted and shook his head. "But if that thing out there was a ship with powers we can't even guess, it might decide to come back. And this time it might not be satisfied with ripping off a bubble."

Bob considered that as he tried to get to sleep. Now he began to hope that Rokoff and his father were right.

3 / Ganymede Colony

THERE WAS NO FURTHER sign of trouble, however, as the next eight days passed and they began to draw up to the orbit of Jupiter. Bob received a note from Andrews the next morning after the trouble, saying that the Captain was happy to grant him the full freedom of the ship. It was a gesture of gratitude that did much to relieve whatever hard feelings he had over his story's reception. Most of the passengers were supposed to stay out of Control. C578439 co. SCHOOLS

Red was up there more often now, on his off-duty periods, staring out at the growing globe that was Jupiter. It was a fantastic sight. Saturn had been disappointing. From Earth, the rings of that planet were gorgeously colored bands, but from nearby they had almost disappeared, turning into nothing but a swarm of ice and rock fragments.

Jupiter became more interesting the closer they came. The huge planet—one-tenth the diameter of the sun—was a blaze of color. The flattening of the poles produced by its rapid rotation could be seen clearly, as could the great bands of color that circled it in every shade from yellow through orange to murky red. The belts and zones were not as clearly separated as the pictures he'd seen, but he could make them out.

Andrews was something of an amateur astronomer, and he proved a more interesting guide to the giant planet than Red, who took too much for granted. The navigator pointed out the great Red Spot that was still a mystery to science after a century of study.

It was located south of the equator, a brick red that stood out strongly as they drew near. It seemed to be rotating with the planet, but Bob knew this wasn't quite true. With time, it moved about over the surface, not keeping up with the rotation of the atmosphere. He remembered that it was some thirty thousand miles long and eight thousand across, covering more area than all the surface of Earth.

"Every time they get a spectroscopic study of it from space or one of the moons, the results are different," Andrews told him. "I guess most astronomers still think it's some kind of light, solid substance floating in the atmosphere, but nobody is sure of anything now."

"It would have to be pretty light," Bob decided. "If it floats in methane gas, it must be lighter than any solid I know."

"Not necessarily. That gas is highly compressed. A few hundred miles down, it becomes pretty heavy. For all we know, you might float above the surface of Jupiter, if there is a surface."

Red was staring out, too. He seemed more interested in the moons that were still small globes around the planet, but he nodded at Andrews' lecture.

"The spot disappeared a few years ago," he added. "It

was there, and then it went away for three years. No trace of it. Four years ago, it came back."

"It has disappeared several times," Andrews said. "First time was in 1919 to 1926. And it gets in trouble at other times. The South Tropical Disturbance—that swirl over there—overtakes the Spot every other year and drags it along for a ways. When that happens, the Spot turns dark. Nobody has figured out why. But it makes great material for the fantasy writers, who keep putting strange races of Jovians there. They make the Spot sound like a big moving continent. And for all I know, they may be right."

But he was smiling as he said it, and Bob knew he didn't really believe in life on Jupiter. Nobody did, of course. It seemed impossible for any life to exist in such an improbable environment.

Twelve hours out from Jupiter, the *Procyon* turned over and began decelerating, cutting its fantastic speed for landing. Most big ships could not land on a planet, since they were too lightly built to stand the weight, but the *Procyon* was braced by the great motors, and it could even land on the oceans of Earth.

Rokoff was taking no chances. Normally, the fields in the ceilings were cut off when under power, but this time he left them on. He was distrustful of all the field installation, and didn't want to try adjusting it. That put both the pressure of the field and the deceleration together to produce what seemed to be double normal weight. Bob labored under it, but soon adjusted. He noticed that it was harder for his father.

"I guess I'm getting old," Dr. Wilson said, and the smile

was uncertain. "I used to take more than this on the old ships. But I'm soft now." He looked tired and strained, and spent most of the time lying down.

The ship roared with the sound of the drive motors. There were no rockets blazing, but power was being sent out in enormous quantities. Somehow, the great drive operated directly against the gravity field of the whole universe. Someday such a drive would take men to the stars, when a better source of power than hydrogen fusion could be found. But that was still far in the future.

Ganymede began to grow on the screen as they passed the outer orbit of Callisto. There was no sign of life that Bob could see, though Red pointed out the place on the moon where he had been born. The planetoid was larger than the Moon of Earth, but it lacked most of the features, craters, mountains, and other marks that Bob had been used to. Its surface was broken into low ranges of hills or mountains and rough plains, but none were very spectacular. The surface itself was rough and rocky, he remembered, but it seemed to be nothing but a desolate waste.

Then they were over Outpost, the colony on the little world. From space, it showed as nothing but a huddle of rounded houses and long enclosed tubes connecting some of them. Beyond lay traces of color that must be the areas where the strange native plants were grown. Everything looked dim and forbidding under the weak light of the sun. It was a gray, unappealing world, and Bob couldn't see why Red wanted to return to it.

He went down with his friend, however. Red couldn't wait until the landing to reach the exit port. He had packed his few belongings, and Bob helped him carry them. The Chief Steward grinned at the boys, but made no objection. as they took up positions in front of the exit.

There was no bump from the landing. The protective field also acted as a cushion as they touched ground. The loud-speaker announced the landing while Bob was still waiting for contact, and the exit began opening.

Red pulled the helmet down on his spacesuit, and Bob followed his example. There was no air on the surface of Ganymede: its gravity had been too weak to hold air. The air in the lock was pumped back, and the inner seal cut them off from the ship, while the outer seal swung all the way open.

Red's mouth was moving as if he were shouting, but no sound could carry without air. He ran forward, throwing his arms around a man with gray hair and a heavy, wrinkled face. Beside the two, a young girl of about eight was bouncing up and down in her spacesuit, trying to attract his attention. A moment later, Red turned to her and gathered her up in his arms, motioning for Bob to join them.

The older man reached out and clamped a small case to the side of Bob's helmet. It must have been some kind of a radio, since a babble of sound reached his ears through the helmet. There were squeals of delight in the girl's voice and something teasing from Red. But it was the older man's words that reached Bob.

"Welcome to Ganymede, Robert. Red has just been telling us he had a friend on board. I'm his uncle—Frank McCarthy, the only doctor on this benighted little world. And this is my daughter Penny."

Penny held out her hand shyly, embarrassed at meeting

a stranger. New faces must have been rare here. But she managed to smile and say hello.

"Are you coming with us?" she asked.

Bob saw that Dr. McCarthy was gathering up the luggage and taking it to a little tractor with an enclosed cabin. They had landed on a cleared section of the planet, a couple of miles beyond the colony of Outpost. Apparently, this was the landing field, since there was a single big shed that must house repair equipment.

"I don't think so, Penny," he told her. "I've got to get back to my father."

Dr. McCarthy nodded. "Give him my greetings, Robert. He'll possibly remember me." At Bob's surprised look, the doctor smiled. "Your father was here years ago studying our plants," he explained. "Tell him I'm still in the same house, and I'll expect both of you for dinner."

Bob watched them going off, suddenly feeling lonely. Now that he'd gotten over his nonsensical ideas about Red, he had grown very much attached to the other boy. He'd miss him on the rest of the long trip back.

He joined Andrews as the navigator moved about. Rokoff was busy with a dark, heavy man who seemed to be the mayor or governor of Outpost, and whose name was Sanchez. The mayor didn't look happy as he received word of what had happened to the bubble containing the supplies intended for the colony, but he shrugged finally as if accepting another piece of the bad luck that always seemed to haunt the colonies.

Andrews was making an inspection of the damaged part of the hull. He had no real duties here, since the First Officer was supervising the instructions for repairs. "Looks like we'll be here three or four days," he decided. "They don't have much equipment for working on a ship like this. We'll probably have to do most of the work ourselves. I'm going back inside. Coming?"

Bob nodded and joined him. Inside, there was a bustle of activity as the stores of the ship were being examined to see how much could be spared to replace the lost stores in the bubble.

Dr. Wilson seemed surprised and pleased to learn that McCarthy was still on Outpost. "He came out as a young doctor with his sister—Bob's mother. When I was here twenty years ago, he was going back to Earth to specialize in extraterrestrial spore diseases. I guess he must have decided he liked it here, after all."

Bob's father still looked tired. Bob studied him worriedly. There was a tradition that all the Wilsons were the healthiest men in the world and that they never got sick. With the exception of one minor case of flu, Bob had been singularly healthy, and he could remember no time when his father had been sick. But the older man didn't look well now.

He looked better, however, as they rode in toward the colony that evening. Dr. McCarthy was driving, pointing out the sights. There didn't appear to be much to see, but he seemed proud of the settlement.

The fields Bob had seen were just that—large cultivated areas. Once a week, pipes below the surface conducted steam out to the ground, where it promptly froze into ice. The plants needed only tiny amounts of the frozen water, and even less of the minerals that were used as fertilizer. They seemed to grow into low, sprawling shrubs, with dark-green patches that served as leaves. How they could exist at two hundred degrees below freezing was a long, involved story of special adaptation by which they bonded the water they needed with other chemicals to make something that remained liquid enough for their life processes. They grew very slowly, though no other plants were as efficient at getting the energy out of what little sunlight they received.

But it was not the larger plants that supported the colony. Those were only fodder for big vats where other one-celled forms of microscopic life broke them down into strange chemicals. Some of those were invaluable to Earth. One was the only antibiotic ever discovered to which no Earth bacteria could develop immunity, and it was the chief export of the colony.

The vats and sheds that held them were only low, ugly affairs, however, and Bob could find nothing interesting there.

The city itself was little more exciting. There were about three thousand people living on Ganymede. Five hundred of those spent their time out prospecting for more plants and what few ores could be found. The rest lived in Outpost, filling about seven hundred of the huts Bob had seen. These were partly dug into the surface, with upper sections that looked like enlarged igloos. There were no windows, but an airlock projected out from each. Some were connected by covered passages. It was pretty primitive, Bob decided, and he wondered how people could live like that.

The interior of Dr. McCarthy's house surprised him, however. It was far larger than it seemed, occupying two levels. The living section was just below ground level, with kitchen, dining room, parlor, and the doctor's office. Below that were a dozen bedrooms, intended to be used for sick patients as well as for the family.

Mrs. McCarthy was a short, plump woman with a red face and a beaming smile. She dried her hands on her apron and greeted Bob warmly. Her voice was soft and seemed filled with the sheer joy of living and cooking and watching her family eat. "Sit down," she told them. "You must be starved after all those space rations. Bob, you sit right here. And Penny, you let him alone, you hear?"

The dinner was obviously a source of pride to her, and it tasted good, though the food was much plainer than that on the ship. But she obviously was a superb cook—only a few people had mastered the knack of making the yeast synthetics taste like real meat.

The two older men were talking about the lost supply bubble. Penny kept trying to break in, but the doctor shushed her good-naturedly, and finally she sat back, pouting a little.

"I do too know what got it," she repeated.

"Shush, child," Mrs. McCarthy ordered quietly. "Eat, or there'll be none of that candy Red brought you. I mean it!"

Surprisingly, Penny quieted.

Dr. McCarthy was obviously worried about the missing supplies, though he tried to cover it up. "I suppose we'll get an emergency shipment in time," he explained. "Since it was lost by accident, Earth should send out one of the unmanned supply rockets. They can make the trip in a few weeks, since they take high acceleration. And it won't be billed against us, at least. That's the government's responsibility. We can get along without uranium for our power pile long enough, I suppose, by reprocessing the slugs we have. We'll make out."

"The ship's collecting all the supplies it can to make up for the other things," Bob told him.

McCarthy nodded. "I know. Captain Rokoff's as good a man as you'll find in space. Unfortunately, though, we're about out of a couple of vitamins, including vitamin C. And the ship doesn't have much of that. For some reason, we need a large dose of that to stay healthy here."

"Maybe you should have gone back to Earth with me years ago. Then you wouldn't have these troubles," Dr. Wilson told him.

McCarthy grinned. "I'm still going back. Just as soon as I can get some other competent doctor for this place. Any day now." He grinned again, taking another slice of cake. "We're beginning to grow, Noel. I figure in another ten years, maybe we'll be large enough to establish another city here."

After the dinner was over, Red took Bob down to the room that was already set up. The furniture was crude, made out of compressed plant fibers and obviously fabricated locally. But it looked comfortable, and there was a large collection of books along one wall. Bob saw that three of them had been written by his father.

Red nodded. "Your father's work is the best I've found yet. He seems to understand our plants. Someday, though, I hope to find a lot more. I'll bet there are hundreds of drugs we could find if we knew how to produce enough of them.

And more commerce is what we need to keep Ganymede growing."

"You really like it here?" Bob couldn't see why, though he knew that the other's values must be different from his.

"It's the best place in the System," Red told him without any doubt. "I've been on Mars, on your Moon, and on Earth. I wouldn't trade the whole lot for Ganymede." Then he grinned. "Of course, without Earth I suppose we couldn't keep going. But Mars started that way, and she's self-sustaining now. Someday we'll be able to stand on our own feet, too."

Bob turned to examine the heavy working vacuum suit standing in one corner. He whistled, realizing now that Red had been right. Wearing it should develop muscles. Instead of being made of plastic and fabric, it was solid metal, with the joints carefully articulated.

"They make them of light alloys," Red told him. "But we use these old-fashioned ones because we need to keep our muscles exercised. Want to try it on? I can let it out here and here so it will fit you."

Bob had his doubts. He wasn't sure he could move around in it, even on this light world. He was saved from the decision by a knock on the door.

It was Mrs. McCarthy, and her face was shocked and unhappy. "Bob!" she said sharply. "Come quickly! It's your father."

Bob broke out of the room at a run, with the other two behind him. There was hardly time for fear to hit at him, however, before he was back in the parlor.

Dr. McCarthy was bending over the figure of Bob's father. The scientist lay on a couch, breathing harshly, and his face was deathly white. He was obviously unconscious.

"It's a stroke—I think a minor one," McCarthy told Bob at once. "He started to come in here for a smoke and keeled over in a faint at the door. Maude and I got him up here, and I've done what I can. But you'd better go for your ship's surgeon. Red will take you."

"He'll live?" Bob asked.

McCarthy nodded. "He'll live, Bob. It isn't that bad, and we can treat these things now. But get going!"

Later, Dr. Jennings from the ship confirmed the diagnosis. By then, Bob's father was conscious again. But his face was still gray. One hand seemed stiff.

"Partial paralysis, Noel," McCarthy told him. "We'll dissolve the clot and get rid of that before any permanent damage. But you take it easy."

"Never been sick a day in my life," Dr. Wilson protested.

"Well, you're going to have to learn how to be now," Jennings told him. "You want the full story? Yes, I thought you would. You've got atherosclerosis—fat deposits in your blood vessels—and your pressure has been going up, probably for years. That strain of landing probably started this, and now you've had a mild stroke. You've been rushing about from planet to planet for years, eating rations and expedition food and getting nowhere nearly enough rest. Now it has caught up with you."

"Will he be all right in time for take-off?" Bob asked.

Jennings and McCarthy exchanged glances. "We'll see," the ship's doctor said. But he sounded doubtful.

4 / Abandoned

DR. WILSON WAS MAKING a speedy recovery, as both doctors told Bob. Jennings went into more details the next day.

"You don't have to worry about a recurrence," he assured Bob. "We'll clear up the cause and bring the pressure down. The brain lesion will heal, and there is no sign of permanent damage. After that, your father will be as sound as ever. But it takes time. A hundred years ago, we couldn't have made a promise like that, so you're lucky. And you can thank one of the drugs made right here for it."

But he wouldn't say whether they could leave or not. He took X-rays, and he and McCarthy studied them carefully. Another day came and went while men from the ship came out on brief visits. Dr. Wilson was a little weak, but he seemed much better, and the paralysis was almost wholly gone.

On the third day, McCarthy reported to Bob and his father together. "It looks as if you're going to be my permanent guest, Noel," he said. "You can't go on. Your brain lesion is doing well, but that pressure is going to take time to bring down. And I don't want you under any strain—not even under the gravity pressure of the ship or of Earth. Here, just as on your own Moon, you have only one-sixth the pressure operating on you, and that makes it a lot easier for your heart and blood vessels to keep the circulation going without building up too much internal pressure. Maybe in a couple of years you can leave. But I don't advise it. We've found that low gravity is the best treatment."

For a long moment, Wilson studied the floor before him. Then he looked up and nodded. "All right, Frank. You're the doctor. Is there any work I can do here?"

McCarthy laughed for the first time in days. "Is there? We could use a dozen men with your ability, Noel! In fact, if I'd had the brains, I'd have doped you and faked this attack twenty years ago. You'll get regular wages. Then you can either stay on as a boarder, or we'll find you a house."

He went out beaming. Dr. Wilson stared at his son, his own face sobering.

"I really don't mind staying," he said slowly. "But I know it's hard for you. Don't go acting noble, son! I know you're thinking of your college. You should think of yourself as well as me. But I don't see what we can do about it."

He tried to explain. He'd never bothered Bob about his finances. They had always had enough to live on, and that had been all Bob cared to know. But now a family council was in order. As holder of a chair at the University, Dr. Wilson had gotten Bob's tuition free. That would end now—he could probably make such an arrangement, but it wouldn't be ethical. And there would still be a great many expenses.

"I had a few savings," he said. "But I'm not a good businessman, Bob. Just before we left, I found my investments were worth nothing. That's the real reason I insisted on taking you along—I couldn't afford to board you out. And on what the colonists can pay me, I couldn't hope to send you to school."

"I'll get used to it, Dad," Bob said. He tried to sound as if it didn't matter. But neither was fooled.

He went to the room he had been assigned. Mrs. McCarthy patted his arm as he went by. The room was comfortable, and he saw that everything of his had already been brought over from the ship. There was even the computer he'd received for his fifteenth birthday, all plugged in and ready to operate. There were the books he'd meant to study and somehow neglected. And there was an end to everything he had planned for at least ten years.

Red came in later. "I heard," he said. "I'm sorry for you, but I'm glad you're staying, Bob. We'll make a real colonist of you. What was that funny subject you were studying?"

"Applied linguistics," Bob told him. He tried to explain it and make the fascination of it obvious. So far, he'd only found a few others who could see it, however, and they had all been in his classes.

In centuries past, men had taken language for granted, though speech was the most remarkable tool ever devised by man. There had been a study called comparative philology, but all that did was to examine the little differences between the human languages—and all of them were much more alike than their differences suggested. It wasn't until the development of machines that could think that a real study could be undertaken of how language worked. Men had to develop a new speech, based on mathematics, to feed information to the computers. And that language had grown by necessity. It was a different type of language. But it suggested that there might be even better methods of speech possible, and they had been groping toward such methods. Loglan III was an artificial speech that showed some promise, but even it was not what they wanted. Men were limited by their speech habits. So were machines limited by the information medium. Somehow, there should be a possible language that would be so logical that it was almost self-evident and perfect for computers, but still so rich that it could express all the wonder and poetry men alone could feel.

"Our trouble is that we have only human languages—even mathematics has a human basis," Bob finished. "We really need a non-human speech for comparison, to find what language really is. But since we don't have that, we have to keep trying to build one. I've got some theories, but I don't know enough yet to test them."

"Yeah." Red shook his head doubtfully. "I can't see it, but I guess you can't see how I feel about using those plants out in the fields—or how Andrews feels about space. Uncle Frank's that way about medicine—if he couldn't be a doctor, I think he'd stop living. Well, maybe in a couple of years you can go back and finish."

Bob nodded, but he didn't believe it. In two years, his class would have gone on. This was a fast-growing science where even two years delay could put him too far behind to catch up—and there was no assurance that it would be only two years.

He tried to read his books, but the intricate puzzle of speech couldn't hold his mind. He knew he was being selfish in worrying about himself, but he couldn't help it. And he also knew there was nothing he could do but accept what he had to do and try to keep from making others miserable over his personal misfortune. Darn it, he should be happy just having the assurance that his father would recover.

Finally he put on the spacesuit and went out to look at the little world that was to be his. It wasn't much to see. There had been three times as many students at the University as there were people on this whole world. And the next place of human habitation was Mars, more than three hundred million miles away. Earth was still farther—so far that it took thirty-five minutes for a radio signal to reach there, even when Earth and Jupiter were closest together!

Most of the people he saw had already met him or knew about him. He was surprised at first when everyone called him by name and greeted him as if he'd been a friend for life. In a few minutes, he caught the feeling of it and was waving and calling out as soon as he saw anyone else.

A surprising number of the people were past fifty. There were some children under ten, but few of his own age. He remembered now that the colony had gone through a very rough period. It had been started out with great hopes after the discovery of the plants and drugs, but most of those who settled had been single men who hoped to make a fortune and go back to Earth. And those with children had sent them back there for an education, and most had remained. It was only in the last few years that the little colony had finally reached a stage where those who came meant to remain. The government had even been forced to pay for their passage, in order to get enough people here. Probably only those who failed on Earth really wanted to settle here. But now the colony was almost large enough to carry on by itself. Experience had proved that any colony of more than five thousand would stop losing most of its younger people and would begin to grow. This was the critical period for Outpost, it seemed.

How could anyone stay, though, he wondered. There was no amusement possible except for radio entertainment beamed out from Earth when conditions were favorable. There wasn't even television. There were no stores—only a community storage center, where every man checked out what he needed, and some kind of accounting was made at the end of the season.

The houses and the plants where the drug processing went on were all set in a small circle, less than a mile in radius. Beyond that, the "farms" stretched out for seven miles to the south, while barren, rocky gulches covered the area to the north. To the east and west, lay low hills that put Outpost in a little valley.

He stared upwards toward where Jupiter seemed eight times as large in the sky as the Moon appeared from Earth. The sun would soon be setting, but the big planet seemed brighter than ever, gleaming with a riot of colors that illuminated the faint shadows cast by the Sun. It was a thrilling sight now. But how long could a man get much thrill out of watching Jupiter?

His wanderings finally brought him out toward the landing field where work had almost been finished on the *Procyon*. He stood back watching that, surprised at how capable the men from Outpost seemed to be in handling the details of repair. Andrews came over to express his sympathy, and Bob asked him about that.

"Most of the older men here were spacemen once," Andrews said. "They would spend maybe ten or fifteen years on the ships, and by that time they were getting too old for space in those days. Until ships were improved, it took young men. Then they'd try to retire to Earth, but they never seemed to like it. So eventually they would drift out, working their passage. Mars got them for a while, until it grew too settled. Then they began coming here. I'm thinking of joining up someday myself, unless we get Titan opened up by then."

Rokoff came over to where they were standing. "Hi, Bob. Tough about your father. And here I thought we were going to make a crewman of you before we got back to Earth."

"Not much chance, I'm afraid, sir," Bob answered, trying to laugh at what was obviously a joke. "I see things that aren't there. You couldn't trust me."

Rokoff grinned and then sobered. "That's right. But I'll tell you—unofficially—that I wouldn't trust a man in space who never saw more than was there. This is no job for men without imagination. Did Mr. Andrews tell you we'd like you and your father for breakfast tomorrow?"

Andrews filled Bob in. It was traditional that when an officer left the ship, he received a farewell. And since Bob had acted as an officer for a few minutes, being the only man on the bridge, he was automatically entitled to the final feast. Anyhow, the science staff wanted to say good-by to Dr. Wilson, so they'd have a breakfast combining officers and scientists. Then they would be taking off at nine in the morning.

53

That meant nine o'clock by standard Greenwich Earth time, since space used that as its basis for measuring days.

It was meant as a gala feast, and it almost succeeded. Most of the time, Bob could forget himself and join in. He'd never heard Rokoff or the First Officer telling jokes before and was surprised at how witty they could be. Even the usually contrived humor of Dr. Wang seemed brighter. And the food was all that any man could ask. It was the special frozen rations shipped out for holidays, including genuine turkey with cranberry sauce.

Bob watched his father carefully, but Dr. Wilson seemed remarkably improved. At times there was a faint awkwardness as he moved his right hand, but it would never have been noticed by anyone who didn't know him well. He saw Jennings watching his father, too, but felt relieved when the doctor smiled and nodded encouragingly. Dr. Wilson even made a short speech, explaining how he had decided it was time to stop chasing after strange life and settle down where strange life could chase him around. It wasn't the most brilliant speech Bob had heard him make, but it seemed to please everyone.

There were presents with the dessert. The men had rifled their own stores to find tobacco and other small luxuries for Dr. Wilson. There were books and bits of scientific equipment whose purpose Bob couldn't even guess. And finally, there was a small portable electron microscope, complete with pump and control panel. That had been the pride of Dr. Swensen, but Wang and the others had chipped in to buy it from him.

"The only one beyond Mars," Dr. Wang said proudly.

"We expect you to go on chasing life, you see. And someday, when you come back to us, we'll get you a whole laboratory of these."

Bob wasn't neglected. Andrews had contributed a whole set of books on higher mathematics, with a carefully worked out schedule of study. He must have lost a whole night's sleep in working that out. There was candy, books, and other small items—enough to form a heavy package.

But at last it was over. Rather awkwardly, Bob and his father moved out to stand beside the equipment that had already been moved outside by others. There was the long whistle indicating the ship was about to be sealed. A few hands waved from the exit port and then withdrew. The ramp moved up, and the outer seal closed.

From inside, there began the roar of the great motors, which, carried through the ship and ground, reached the soles of their shoes first, before it could travel through the air of their suits to their ears.

The *Procyon* lifted slowly on her protective field. When she was two feet off the ground, the great drive came on. There was no wash of flame from the rear nor any outward sign that she was pouring out power. There seemed only a faint distortion of the space around her and a feeling of vague pressure.

Then she began to rise, tilting her nose upwards as she reached the thousand-foot level. There full power must have been applied, and the *Procyon* began to lift into space and head for Earth.

McCarthy and Red were in the tractor, waiting. They had loaded the gifts while the ship was first lifting. But Bob and his father waited outside, following the take-off of the huge metal monster that had been their home for months.

It was dwindling now as it picked up thirty-two feet of speed per second for every second its motors worked. In a minute, it was growing small. In four minutes, it was hard to see against the black of space. Then there were only faint indications as it temporarily blotted out a star here or there. Even that became impossible to see, but still Bob strained his eyes, fancying he could make out a tiny spot.

He felt tears in his eyes. Three hundred and fifty million miles away lay Earth, rich with everything he had dreamed of, and full of promise. It was less than a month's trip for the *Procyon*, or perhaps six months for any other ship. But it might as well have been light years for Bob.

His father's arm went over his shoulder, and he glanced up, trying to keep his face turned to hide the tears. He needn't have bothered. There were unashamed tears in his father's eyes, too. For the older man, Earth must also have meant a great deal. It had meant a degree of fame, association with his colleagues, the latest gossip of science, and opportunities no other world could have provided.

Dr. Wilson managed to smile as he turned toward the waiting tractor. "All right, son," he said. "We've had our fun. Now I guess it's time to go home and go to work."

Home! Bob choked on the word.

5 / Wild Tales

MRS. MC CARTHY SEEMED SURE that they couldn't have had
enough to eat on the ship, and she had breakfast waiting. Bob
and his father tried to make her happy, but it was too much.
Eventually, they settled for coffee before storing their pos-
sessions in their rooms. They had decided to stay on with
Dr. McCarthy, paying him for lodging. Neither knew too
much about housekeeping, and they were sure they couldn't
do better. Besides, Mrs. McCarthy seemed happy to take on
the extra burden.

"When can I start working, Frank?" Dr. Wilson asked.

The doctor shrugged. "Whenever you like, if you'll take
it easy and promise to rest whenever you feel tired. We've
found that a little work is better for a man than brooding."

"Then suppose I set up my things in a spare corner of
some shop today."

They went out, with Bob following. He had no desire
to be alone with his thoughts. The spare corner turned out to
be rather more than that. The colonists had cleaned out a
whole floor of one of their underground shops and made it
ready for Wilson. The microscope was already mounted on

a bench, and a fair amount of equipment had been assembled. Red was waiting beside it.

"It was my father's laboratory," he said. "We'd like you to have it, Dr. Wilson."

McCarthy nodded. "We couldn't be happier to see you here, Noel. Jim Mullins—Red's father—was a first-rate chemical engineer, and it was he who pretty much helped us start growing with what he learned. But maybe a good biochemist who understands Gany life is even better. We sort of hoped Red would be your assistant."

"Oh?" Wilson studied the boy with new interest. "Well, I need a helper, though Bob has sometimes worked with me. What are your qualifications, Red?"

"I studied under my father. Then I had two years of advanced study under Professor Mubuto at St. Louis. He let me skip the elementary courses, so it was all post-grad work, even though I'd never had a bachelor's degree."

"Umm." The name of Mubuto obviously impressed Wilson, but he stared critically at the young man before him. "Aren't you a little young for all that?"

"I got started young—I had to, sir."

Wilson laughed. "Okay, Red. I'll buy that, and you're hired. You'll probably have to teach me until I find out what's needed here. What's the biggest problem now?"

McCarthy nodded to Bob and they left the two others busy with technical talk. Bob had taken it for granted that he would be assigned work helping his father. He felt a touch of bitterness at seeing another replace him, though he had to admit that Red was probably much better qualified.

"And what do I do?" he asked McCarthy.

58

The doctor shrugged. "Pretty much what you want, or what you can do. You're still a minor, and your father's working, so you can do nothing, if you like."

"I'd rather find something to do."

"Good!" McCarthy quickened his pace. "I'm glad you decided that, Bob. This place doesn't like slackers, though you're not compelled to work. But we're too close to the ragged edge of disaster here at all times to be able to afford idleness. We get a few things shipped out from Earth, but the freight is high, even when you consider that our drugs bring high prices. And the ships can make this long trip only about twice a year. So we have to make almost everything ourselves. That's why we need every effort from every man here. I'll take you in to see Mayor Sanchez and let him decide what you can do."

The Mayor also beamed when Bob asked for work. He pulled Bob into the little room that served as his office and began quizzing him. Sanchez was obviously not a very highly educated man—he bragged that he'd been only a common spaceman—but he had a quick native intelligence. It took him about five minutes to weed out all the things that Bob could and couldn't do.

"Mostly you'd need training here, see?" he explained. "I don't say you can't learn quick. You got a good mind. So you can learn, once you find something you really want to try. But right now, you don't know about plants, you don't know enough chemistry, you can't farm, and you can't mine. Sure, manual labor—but you gotta get used to handling a vac suit first. Tell you what, I can use you as a clerk. Keep records of things like how much mayweed we plant, how much we get for how much fertilizer, what prices are, figure out what we do best at. Okay?"

"Okay. But I thought your son was already doing that work."

"Good boy! Sure, but I'm not fooling you." Sanchez let out a yell, and a smaller, fairer edition of himself came in. "Pete, this is Bob. He's gonna learn what you do. Bob, Pete wants to be a farmer for a while, and we need that. I been keeping him here looking for a clerk, so now you're it."

Pete began showing Bob around the office and filing room. It was hardly an efficient setup. There was a battered typewriter and an ancient hand-operated calculator that could only add and subtract. But nothing about the job seemed too hard.

"Don't worry, Bob," Pete told him. "Dad doesn't play around. When he says he can use you, he means it. Of course, it's about the lowest job in the colony. That's why he assigned it to me, because I'm his son. But we all have to start somewhere."

Bob grimaced to himself. On the way out to Titan, he'd felt that Red somehow wasn't quite his social equal because the other was a steward and a colonial. Now the tables were turned. They still weren't social equals, but now Bob was the underdog.

"Okay," he said. "How do I start somewhere?"

Actually, the job wasn't too hard. Pete had a total contempt for system, but Bob began to get the feel of things. He brought in his own typewriter and calculator and began putting the files into a regular order. In that, he was lucky.

He'd had basic filing theory when working at tabulating statistics about language studies.

Pete left the third day, satisfied that Bob could take over. And for that day, there was some feeling of satisfaction. But it began to fade quickly. The job was too easy. Work that had taken days on the old machine went through his computer in hours. The work was mostly designed to keep tabs on what production should be, and that could be done in advance. Bob could see that in three weeks he would be out of work for the next six months, though he would have to stay on, since he had to be available at all times for anyone who wanted information. It was going to be the biggest bore of all time, unless he was mistaken.

Even Penny's job seemed more interesting. She was sent out three hours a day, when not in school, to check the plants for wilted stalks. Most of the children did some work such as that. Even Mrs. McCarthy worked in one of the processing plants.

Bob tried to study his books, but he found it slow going. With no hope of getting anywhere, he had a hard time making himself open them. It all seemed pointless.

It was Saturday afternoon and his fifth day when Sanchez came in. He looked over the neatly arranged office and filing room and nodded. "See? I pick 'em good, eh? Payday, young man. You want to get paid?"

Bob considered it. He'd learned that Sanchez didn't ask stupid questions. Naturally, a worker would want his pay. But if it had been so natural, Sanchez would have paid him and not asked.

"What happens if I don't?" he asked.

"Same as with most of us. If you got some reason for money—something you need from Earth, say—we pay whatever we can. If not, you get credit—not any exact amount, just credit. Then you take what you need. If you start taking too much, we tell you. If not, it's your business. We don't have much cash sometimes. That has to be saved for trade."

"Okay, I don't need to be paid," Bob decided. He couldn't think of any legitimate use for money anyway in a place that had no regular shops.

Sanchez nodded heavy approval. "Good boy. We'll make a Ganyman of you yet. In that case, you go to stores and get yourself a real vac suit. That thing they let you have from the ship isn't safe. Fall over and scratch it and it rips. Then you try breathing nothing. People die that way."

There was an older man in the store looking over some rebuilt tools when Bob went in. He saw half a dozen of the vacuum suits stacked along one wall and he moved toward them, studying them. There were larger stores of bottled oxygen, along with the big pump that compressed the gas for them. He stopped, trying to make up his mind.

"Hi, Bob," the older man said. "I'm Dan Kirby. Looking for a suit?"

He reached over and picked one up easily, though it must have weighed well over a hundred pounds, even on Ganymede. "This one is a good one. Used to be Tom Bailey's until he got lost prospecting. Darned fool. I told him to stay off the other side. But it's a nice suit, and it should fit. Ever been in one before?"

"No," Bob admitted. He realized it was a lot more suit than any he had tried.

Under Kirby's direction, he got into it somehow. The back hinged out and then locked against a seal. Kirby adjusted it for his size after it was on and showed him how to pass the straps over his shoulders to carry the weight most comfortably. Two bottles of oxygen slipped into place, while Kirby made sure he could handle the controls.

"Now walk," the old farmer suggested.

Bob started to take a step. Nothing happened. He lifted again, and this time he felt his leg rise. It was like swimming in molasses.

The suit had only a hundred and thirty pounds of weight, but it had about eight hundred pounds of inertia. Getting motion started was like trying to move a heavy sled on ice—it resisted until it reached speed, and then resisted any effort to stop.

He took a second step, and his leg went on moving. There was a dull thud as he hit the floor, and Kirby was reaching down to help him up.

"Reminds me of when I first wore a suit like this, patching tubes on the old *Michigan*," he said. "But you'll learn."

"The *Michigan*?" The space ships named for states hadn't been in use for decades. Kirby couldn't be that old, even if he had signed on as a young cabin boy for the last voyage.

"Sure. Rode her ten years, before I got promoted to the *Ohio*. Great ship for her day. Not like that silly thing you came on. You had to be a *man* in space then. Come on, try it again."

Bob saw no sign of a grin on the old face. That would make Kirby at least ninety years old, however—and probably a good deal more. He'd heard that some of the older men were good at spinning wild tales, however. It was their idea of humor, like the fantastic stories spacemen had once told about Davy Dreadnaught, who could breathe on Mars without a helmet and who once jumped all the way from the Moon to the Earth "because he had to," only to land in Lake Tiwanac; that was why there was no Lake Tiwanac above Superior now—the splash Davy made had left it dry from that day on.

"It still takes good men," Bob said. "Didn't you hear about Captain Rokoff? When the protective field broke down, he had to climb out and keep the meteors off with a baseball bat. He lost three pounds in ten minutes running around the hull."

Kirby grinned slowly. "You're a good kid, but you're an awful liar. That story's so old I'd almost forgot it. Come on, keep trying to walk. You're getting the hang of it."

The old man stuck around for almost an hour, giving instructions, and finally walked down the street with Bob toward his home to make sure no trouble would happen to him. At the entrance, he nodded.

"You'll need some more practice before you're good in it, but nobody'll laugh at you now. Go on in and show 'em."

He went off about his own business, leaving a glow of warmth behind, and Bob went in, wading carefully against the inertia of his suit. Kirby was right. Nobody laughed at him, and Mrs. McCarthy assured him he was very good.

Some of his satisfaction evaporated the next day, however, when he saw Penny come out in hers. She walked as casually as if she'd been dressed for a summer stroll on Earth.

"No work today," she told him. "Sunday. Red and your father have to do something, though, and Daddy says he's got a call. So how would you like me to show you Outpost? I know all about it."

He climbed into his suit doubtfully, wondering how long it would be before his shoulders got used to wearing the harness. Then he went out with her. It seemed silly to have to have an eight-year-old girl show him around, but at least it wouldn't be wasting any more valuable time.

It was quite a tour, and Penny really did know Outpost. She took him through the processing plants, where he could see that some men had to attend the vats even on Sunday. Here the one-celled creatures fermented and changed the mess of Ganymedan plants to more salable products. It was crude engineering, but the remarkable thing was that most of it seemed to have been made here somehow.

Penny explained. Everything had to be made here, because it cost so much to ship anything out from Earth. Once they had a lucky strike—a ship crashed on Callisto, and they were able to drag the wreck back with the tug and use everything in it. But mostly they had to mine the metal from ore that was too poor to be worth anything on Earth, to smelt it themselves, and to fabricate everything as best they could.

She showed him the air plant. This was in two sections. In one, oxygen was broken down from ores found on the surface of the moon. Native plants seemed to do most of the work, releasing a slow trickle of the vital gas, though some ore required processing first. The second section was another matter. This was a big greenhouse affair on the hillside west of Outpost. Apparently, all the houses had pipes that led here, and a great garden was growing, turning the carbon dioxide, exhaled by the men, back into oxygen while supplying food at the same time.

Water was broken from other rocks, though a prospector sometimes found some ice under the surface.

It was a world where nothing came easily, as Bob was beginning to learn. The first men to establish the colony must have had more supplies or they could never have existed long enough to learn to live here. Still, he supposed Mars had been colonized in a similar way, though there the temperature and sunlight were more favorable.

He glanced up at Jupiter. The Red Spot loomed immense, and the color bands around the planet seemed to be churning and twisting, as if huge storms were going on there. It reflected almost as much light onto Ganymede as the Sun gave here, though that light was a dull reddish color.

"That's where they came from," Penny said. "I guess they were being bad when they went after you, but they don't mean any harm."

"What are you talking about, Penny?" he asked.

"The men in the big round, white ship," she said. "The one that stole the bubble. I'm going to give it to them for that when I see them."

"You mean you've seen the ship?"

She nodded. "Oh, sure, lots of times. They land back there to the north of us and wait for me. When I can get away, I go out and talk to them. They give me nice things when I can find some metal for them. Of course, nobody else sees them, but I like them."

Bob groaned to himself. It seemed that both the old and the young went in for tall tales here. She must have heard about what Bob saw from Red, and she was making up her own stories now. But he couldn't blame her. Here, with almost nothing to do except study and work, and with only a few kids of her own age, he could see why she had to make fantasy worlds for herself.

"I'm sure they're nice people, Penny," he agreed. "You'll have to show them to me sometime."

"Sure. Only they're scared of strangers. You'll have to be very careful."

Later, he told Red about it, expecting the other boy to laugh. To his surprise, Red frowned. "Penny's funny," he said, "but she's picked up some odd things somewhere. And maybe she did see something like that globe you spotted. At least a couple others here in the colony claim that they've seen a globe passing over."

"You mean you're beginning to believe I saw an alien ship?" Bob asked.

"I don't know," Red told him. "Oh, I don't believe all that you saw, or much of what Penny said. But I've been hearing enough funny things to make me uncomfortable. If there was a ship that attacked the *Procyon* and almost killed us, I'd hate to have it hanging around here. One swipe by that thing at our power pile and we'd be dead before we could get replacements."

6 / Plague Warning

IT TOOK TWO MORE weeks before the last of the work Bob could find to do was completed and the last sight Penny could find had been shown. By then he knew most of the people of the colony, and he found that he liked nearly all of them. They were rough and sometimes uncouth, but they were usually kind. Probably where everyone's life depended on everyone else, the men who behaved badly were soon made so unwelcome that they couldn't stay.

The one really happy thing about the time was the remarkable improvement in Bob's father. Dr. Wilson was back at work full time now, and sometimes had to be pried away from his research. But he looked good, and the doctor admitted that he was in good shape.

His blood pressure had come down almost to normal. At first the quickness of the improvement had puzzled McCarthy, but he began to accept it as good progress. The last sign of the paralysis was gone, and there was no indication of the depression McCarthy had feared.

Bob went over to visit the laboratory when his own work

was finished; Sanchez had chased him out for his own good. "You drive me crazy looking for someone to come in and ask information. Go on, get out. Nobody will have trouble finding you here if they want you. Go get yourself a girl friend."

It was a standard joke. The only girl living on Outpost who was nearly Bob's age was Maria Sanchez. Bob liked her well enough, but he could see that she and Red had already come to an understanding. About the only other girl he saw was Penny, and she was still too young, though she seemed unaware of it sometimes. Probably to her, he represented the glamor of Earth. And besides, he still had some candy left from the presents he'd received.

He found Red and his father busy over a mess of assorted glassware, studying something that was a sickly green and gave off a vile odor. Dr. Wilson was sniffing it as if it were attar of roses.

"What is it?" he asked.

"Grease—or it will be," Wilson answered. "That's something they've lacked here. There is no satisfactory lubricant, and all has to be imported from Earth. But unless I'm mistaken, this culture can produce a vegetable grease out of waste that will be almost as good as the silicone synthetics. It won't sell to Earth—but it will save a lot of freight money, so that what does sell can buy more. All right, Red, you can figure how to get it into bigger production. I think we've got it."

"I still don't see how you guessed it," Red said. He was obviously as happy as Dr. Wilson.

"There are a lot of things that should have been guessed. The trouble is that the native life here hasn't been properly studied for more than fifty years—not since the new methods were worked out."

"Don't forget, you studied it yourself twenty years ago," Bob reminded him.

Wilson chuckled. "That's right. But not properly. I was trying to find proof for certain theories important back on Earth, not to see what could be done for the colony. I have a feeling Red and I can put things on a financially solvent basis in three more years with what we turn up."

Again Bob felt a brief twinge of jealousy, though he knew it was unjustified. Red was obviously rising steadily in his father's opinion. Logically he knew that Red was earning his way and that he himself couldn't have done the work. But it hurt. Then he forced the idea from his mind.

"I haven't seen you look so good in five years, Dad," he said.

"I haven't felt as good in ten," his father agreed. "Maybe there's something about this place that's just naturally healthy."

Maybe there was, Bob thought. He went out to wander around and see if he could help with harvesting one of the plant growths. In time, he might at least work up to be a farmer that way. It wasn't much, but it would beat clerking.

He finally located the patch Dan Kirby was working. The old farmer waved a greeting and went on, busily scraping something from the underside of the stalks. "Hi, Bob. See you walk pretty good in your suit now?"

"Yeah. Thanks again, Mr. Kirby." Bob had almost forgotten the trouble with the suit. He couldn't handle it as well as Red yet, but he felt at home in it. "What's wrong with the plants?"

"Some blamed pest. Kind of a fungus. At this stage I have to watch them."

Bob hadn't realized that the plants here had pests. Kirby snorted. "Anytime you get something growing well, some kind of ornery life comes along and learns to live off it. They have pests every place I've seen, and I've seen most of them. Reminds me of the time I was on the old *Taft* when we set down on Mars——"

"Wait a minute." Bob stared at the other, but the expected smile wasn't there. "The *Taft* blew up in '13. That's eighty-one years ago."

Kirby nodded. "That so? I guess you're right. Yeah, you're right. I remember I was on the Moon when I heard about it. I'd have been just twenty-two then. Yep, you're right. Anyhow, I got off at Marsport right in the middle of the first attack of Martian fever. We all knew then that Martian bugs didn't attack people. But we forgot that there hadn't been enough people around for the bugs to learn to like 'em. You put food out of any kind, and some pest comes along and takes it."

Bob gave up. If the old man wanted to stick to his story, it was his privilege. "Can I help you, Mr. Kirby? I'm all through at the office."

"That's right nice of you, Bob." Kirby lifted a stalk and pointed. "See that? That's what wilts things. It has to be scraped off. Simple enough, but you have to get all of it."

Bob fell to beside the older man. He felt good about

keeping up with Kirby until he saw that the other was doing three rows while he cared for only one. But Kirby seemed not to notice. It was backbreaking work because of the bending over. But there was nothing too difficult about it.

Kirby stopped at the end of the row and maneuvered a water flask through the trap-door arrangement of his suit. He passed it over to Bob next. "Never realized how good water was till I got here," he said. "So you want me to teach you how to be a farmer, eh?"

Bob hadn't mentioned it, but he grinned. "I had something like that in mind."

"Good idea. You should learn to do everything here. You've got a good head, so you can do it. Then you find what you like best, and settle down to that. Farming's pretty good, too." He returned to the rows of plants. "Reminds me of when Davy Dreadnaught decided to try growing corn on the Moon. Nobody'd ever tried it, figuring corn needed air, but Davy was stubborn. He kept a-working at it, giving it less air and less, until finally he got some that learned how to get along. He planted him a fine crop of it, and it started coming up just grand. Naturally, being on the Moon where no other plants had used up the good in the soil, it started to grow bigger and bigger. This was at night there, and it got to be eighty feet tall just by starlight and earthshine. Got ears fourteen feet long, with kernels bigger than a bushel basket. Davy figgered come daylight, he'd have the finest crop ever grown. But he made him one little mistake."

Bob waited. The old man went on, quietly, scraping off the fungus and humming to himself. Finally Bob gave up. "Okay, what mistake did Davy make?"

72

"Oh, yeah, that. Well, turned out it was popcorn he'd planted. When the Sun came up, the heat popped the whole crop. You can still see all those craters where that corn blasted to bits."

In spite of himself, Bob chuckled. The old man looked up with shrewd eyes. Then he began chuckling himself.

The next day Bob took the trouble of looking up his files. He was somewhat surprised to find that there were vital statistics on everyone there, including himself. He found Kirby's card and stared at it unbelievingly. The age worked out to one hundred and three, just as Kirby had said. And there were citations for bravery in a space accident that had occurred aboard the *Taft!*

The man looked old to Bob, but nowhere nearly that old. He seemed like a remarkably healthy and well-preserved sixty, at most. And there had been nothing frail about his work nor senile in the way he'd spotted Bob's disbelief in his true age, and pulled that Davy Dreadnaught yarn in joking revenge.

Bob began riffling through the whole file now, watching only for the date of birth. He soon found one for a woman over eighty—a Mrs. Steinberg, who'd been in to find out what the best chances were for planting. She had seemed about fifty. Then there was Stefan Gersdansky, who couldn't possibly be the ninety-four the card indicated. This man was the one who operated the blacksmith forge where all the tools were repaired. He looked younger than Bob's father.

There were several more like that. Bob put the files away. His father had said it was a healthy place—but this sounded like something almost unnaturally healthy, unless it was pure coincidence. All the very old were ones who had come to Ganymede long ago. It was almost as if living here had somehow stopped them from aging normally.

He found another file, and then gave up. He'd found enough, without checking through death records to see how old those who died here had been.

Bob found Dr. McCarthy in his office. There was a patient, but she left in a few moments, and the doctor seemed glad to see Bob. He listened to the young man's facts, nodding now and then.

"I never really checked up, but I found the general pattern a long time ago," he said. "You're right. Kirby hasn't changed a bit that I can see in more than twenty years. There's Sanchez, too. When he first came here twenty years ago, he had lung cancer. He was too sick to ship back. I couldn't risk an operation, and there were no drugs available here for the cure they had then on Earth. But two years later, Sanchez was out prospecting, as healthy as you are."

"Then there really is something here that's healthy?" Bob asked.

McCarthy shook his head. "I'm not sure, Bob. I've started to write up a report a dozen times, and then quit. There were the Hungarian peasants Metchnikoff studied. Some of them lived to be a healthy hundred, and he thought they stayed healthy by eating yogurt. Only it didn't help anyone outside their section, and nobody else who went there lived any longer than normal. You get sporadic cases like this. Maybe it's just coincidence, but there's another side to it, too. Here."

74

He swung around and drew out a long sheet of paper. "You can see this, since I haven't listed the patients' names— just a code number. Look it over."

It was the list of his patients for the last three months. Bob went down it. McCarthy, he was sure, was a highly competent doctor. Jennings had treated him with respect, and the school he'd attended was a tough one. But most of the diseases were listed as "Unknown," with a designation after them which was apparently only a private name used by McCarthy. And there were far more cases of sickness than he would have expected from the size of the population.

McCarthy put the sheet back. "Most of the sickness I treat is of a kind I never studied in medical school. Oh, I've found things to help, but I suspect they just cure themselves. We don't have many deaths, but there's a lot of sickness. Mostly it strikes the young people and those who've just come here. I've been expecting you to turn up sick, though you and your father seem to be pretty tough. By the time a man has been here twenty years, he seems to have got pretty well over being sick—or he did until recently. Lately I've been seeing more older people come in, and with worse trouble. So far, they recover. That's one reason I never left here—this place would drive any sane doctor crazy."

"And you never reported it?"

"No. And I've showed this to you so you'll keep your mouth shut, too, Bob. Let word of the old people's age get out and we'd be swamped by senile wrecks who would ruin the colony. Or let the other side out and we'd never get enough colonists. That's why the Martian fever was hushed up—oh, you've heard of that?—well, it was never revealed. I thought they were wrong to hide it, once. Now I'm not so sure. I can't keep you from spreading the word, but I suggest you don't."

Bob nodded. He'd thought he had made a remarkable discovery, but he might have guessed McCarthy would have learned of it before. And with the ethics of the profession and all the years to think of it, if McCarthy hadn't announced it, he didn't feel he should.

"Of course, if we ever got a real plague like Martian fever, that threatened to spread, I'd have to announce it and quarantine Ganymede." McCarthy sighed. "It's worried me at times. But so far, there has never been anything but isolated cases, and no sign of spreading."

Bob went back to the office to sit and wonder. It seemed that Ganymede was no healthier or sicker than most places —people got sick more often and lived longer, but that probably balanced out on the plus side.

He was just closing up to go home for dinner when Sanchez came rushing in. The Mayor was in more of a hurry than Bob had ever seen before. "Bob—Bob, you still there?"

Bob turned on the light, and the Mayor sighed with relief.

"I got a real rough job," he said. "I want you to find out and make up a list showing everyone you, Red Mullins, or your father talked to without a spacesuit on. Starting with me. You begin on your own list—take the sheet giving our population and go down it. I'll get your father and Red in here at once."

He was gone out the entrance so rapidly that the airlock hardly had time to seal behind him. Bob frowned over it and began listing people. There were all the Sanchez family, the McCarthy family. . . . It was quite a list, including Dan Kirby, who had helped him put on his suit.

Red and Dr. Wilson came in fifteen minutes later, puzzled but doing their best to remember. Bob's father had seen fewer people than anyone else, but Red seemed to have associated with everyone.

When he was finished, Sanchez took the list and went down it, muttering unhappily. "Every person on Ganymede except a bunch of prospectors who haven't come back, and Mrs. Lupescu."

"I saw her, come to think of it," Red said.

Sanchez gravely marked the correction. "So between the three of you, you've seen everyone in Outpost. And they want me to quarantine you or something!"

"Who wants you to what?" Dr. Wilson asked. As Dr. McCarthy came in, Dr. Wilson turned toward him, looking for possible clarification. But the doctor had been summoned without being told why.

Sanchez fumbled in his pockets and mopped his brow. Finally he found a piece of paper and spread it out. "This came over the space radio," he said. "About an hour ago. Look."

It was a handwritten scrawl on a radiogram form that was faded from age. Wilson picked it up and read it aloud:

"Starship *Procyon* found to have epidemic raging. Ship in quarantine orbit, epidemic being studied. Believed to be of possible Titan origin, since symptoms previously unknown. Suggest immediate isolation of all who contacted three from expedition."

It was signed by the World Health Officer.

Sanchez shook his head. "How can I isolate everybody?"

"Forget it," McCarthy suggested. "The warning of the plague was a good idea, but they don't realize back there that our whole world isn't much more than a small village. Anyhow, all the exposed are isolated from those not exposed—since there are none of the latter. Wire back that you've complied, and keep him happy."

"But what do we do?"

"Nothing until we see trouble here." McCarthy tore up the telegram and tossed the bits in a basket. "Bob, Red, and Noel here are all healthy, and at least one of them should have been sick by now if the whole ship was infected several days ago—long enough for quarantine orders. It may be something picked up after they left, though I can't see how. But all we can do is wait and see. You'd better get whoever took this message to keep quiet about it, though, or you'll have a panic starting here."

Red grunted. "You'll have it then, Uncle Frank. When I was on the way here, Larry Coccagna was busy showing a yellow slip of paper to a group in front of the storeroom. I'll bet he made a carbon copy of the message."

Sanchez groaned. He slapped down his helmet and went out at a run. But he was back soon after, shaking his head. He had obviously given up trying to stop the spread of the story.

"Maybe you'd better put us all in quarantine for our own protection, Luis," McCarthy said. "With your nephew spreading the story, we may need to be locked up before they decide to lynch us. That's the way things worked on Mars during the fever." He turned to Bob, smiling bitterly. "Maybe you've changed your mind now, young man. This doesn't look like a very healthy place."

7 / The Globe from Space

THE FINAL RESULTS OF the conference in the Mayor's office were that they should all act as if nothing had happened, while McCarthy tried to quiet fears. He gave the three as careful an inspection as he could, so that he could honestly swear that in his opinion there was no sign of plague among them.

"And it's true, so far as I can tell," he said.

It worked better than Bob had expected. There were some hostile signs during the morning as he went to work, and Sanchez had received some alarmed inquiries. But during the day it seemed to blow over.

"We get to be pretty close knit here," Sanchez explained. "What outsiders think isn't too important. And by now, seeing how old Kirby thinks you're the best kid to hit this place and McCarthy thinks your father is about perfect, you're both insiders. They know you and like you, so they don't figure you're contagious."

It didn't seem completely logical to Bob, but he was grateful for it, and secretly greatly pleased to think that Kirby had been saying good things about him. He'd grown quite fond of the old man, though the idea of such an age filled him with awe.

Kirby's tractor drove up to the administration office in mid-afternoon, and the old man got down spryly, to come stomping in. "You finished here, yet, Bob? Sanchez said you could take off, so I dropped by. Had to get me a hoe fixed."

Bob put the cover on the calculator and got up. He found Kirby's vital statistics card and put it down before the old man. Kirby glanced at it, not even squinting as he scanned the fine print. Then he laughed. "So you found out I was telling the truth. Always like to have a little fun with new people about that. But forget it, now that you know. What difference does it make?"

It obviously made none. They were busy hoeing weeds out of the long, stringy vines Kirby called snakeberries, which produced one of the most valuable hormones exported to Earth. "Weeds, too?" Bob asked.

"Bound to be. I grew up on a farm in Arkansas where we had worse ones, though." Kirby stopped to examine the hoe. The frozen, rocky ground was hard to cut, requiring carbide-tipped blades. The plants were almost as tough. The most tender shoot on Ganymede would have made teak wood seem pliant.

"Stands to reason," he went on. "Plants weren't made just for us. They were made to grow any way they could, and we have to take the worst with the best. Sometimes I get to feeling they think we were made for them. Reminds me of the time Davy Dreadnaught tried to grow pumpkins on Mars."

It was a long, rambling story, and one that had never

been collected in the book of Davy Dreadnaught episodes. Bob found himself laughing in spite of himself.

"That's a little like the time Davy found the only tree on Venus, isn't it?" he asked.

"Don't think I heard about that," Kirby said doubtfully. "Go on, I'll stop you if I have."

It was an even longer story, since Bob had discovered already that the trick of such stories was adding as much detail as possible. He expected to be stopped at any moment, since it was one of the first stories in the book, but Kirby listened with fascinated interest. At the end, the old man stopped to roar with joyful laughter.

"That's a good one, boy," he said. Then he sobered a little. "And you see what happened? We got so busy with it, we never even noticed how time went, and we're all done. That's why those stories were invented—to keep a man from going nuts on some long job like chipping tube linings. So don't waste 'em just showing off that you know them."

Bob went back to the McCarthy's house in a fog of physical fatigue, but feeling somehow good. He'd never really done physical work before. Unlike athletics, it left him with a sense of being tired for a real purpose. Mrs. McCarthy beamed over the amount of food he ate.

"Nothing like fresh air," she said, "to give you an appetite."

Bob couldn't see what fresh air had to do with it—since he'd been breathing canned oxygen. But it was a saying she'd kept from her childhood, apparently, and one not to be examined too critically.

McCarthy called them into his office after the meal, to

make a routine examination, but he seemed satisfied. "I don't really think there was any plague from Titan," he said. "But I'd rather not take chances."

"No sign of plague here, anyhow," Red said.

McCarthy wasn't as quick to agree as he might have been. He stopped to fill a pipe and light it. Then he shrugged. "I don't know. There's an increase of sickness here, and some of the cases seem worse. But it's all of a type I've seen before —or seems to be. Maybe there is a plague, but we're all partly immune. From what your expedition dug up, life on Titan seems similar to that on Ganymede, doesn't it, Noel?"

"No." Wilson's reply was less cautious than Bob had expected. Scientists were usually reluctant to make unqualified statements without a lot of evidence. But his father seemed quite sure. "No, Frank, there's no real connection. There's a resemblance, probably because the environment is similar. And both strains show some signs of having originated on Earth millions of years ago. But the life on Titan has an entirely different cellular structure. I don't see how immunity here would help with anything from there."

"Umm." McCarthy frowned. "I was sort of counting on that. I discounted you and Bob, since you both tell me you're naturally resistant to disease. But maybe I'll have to revise my theories now. Oh, well, it's nothing too serious yet."

Bob went to his room, leaving the two older men alone over their pipes. He had to admit that his father seemed to be almost happy here. And at times, he found he liked it too. But he wondered how long his interest in farming would last. The clerical job had grown boring in two weeks. Farming might last a little longer, until the novelty wore off. Then there was mining, processing, maybe even prospecting, if his father would let him try it. But in a year, how would he feel?

He stretched out, resting his tired muscles. Then his eyes fell on his suit. It was badly stained by the bits of weed. He had made it a regular practice to clean off anything on it, and this was no time to get sloppy. He got up and got out the brush and oil to clean it. As he was finishing, there was a soft rap on his door, and Red came in.

The boy dropped a few trinkets on Bob's table. "Look at those."

Bob picked one up. It seemed to be a flat sheet of plastic with colors in a fancy pattern. He turned it over and then face up. It looked completely uninteresting until his hand accidentally squeezed the edge. Then the pattern began to change, like the patterns in a kaleidoscope. But this seemed less random. It was as if lines and colors were performing a dance. As he squeezed harder, the dancing figures speeded up, until there was a blur of colors.

The next object was simply a round ball about two inches in diameter, perfectly polished. It seemed to be glass, but it glittered brilliantly.

"It's a diamond," Red said. "A perfect diamond. I tested it with the spectroscope."

There were a few other things that Bob couldn't identify. "Where did you get them?" he asked.

"In Penny's room. She left her door open a crack, and in the light from the hall, I saw them shining under her bed. I suppose I had no right, but after some of the things she's been saying, I had to find what they were. Well?"

Bob shook his head. Nothing like them had ever been seen, so far as he knew. The diamond ball was obviously artificial, and larger than any diamonds Earth produced. The other things were totally unfamiliar.

"She's been stealing little bits of metal all week, too," Red said. "I caught her taking some of my solder. She seems to like lead best, if she can find it. She wouldn't explain. And now she's sneaked out!"

"You mean she's not in her room?"

"I mean she's sneaked out," Red repeated. "I've checked all over. She used to do that when she was hardly able to walk. She'd pretend to go to sleep, then get into her suit and go wandering. But I thought she'd given up."

Bob reached for his suit and began climbing into it. "I think she may have gone north," he guessed.

"From what she said, I'd guess the same," Red agreed. "We'd better hurry if we want to catch her. But don't let her know we're on her trail, or she'll disappear. There are a lot of gulleys up there, and she knows them better than I do."

Mrs. McCarthy was washing dishes as they came up the stairs. She lifted an inquiring eyebrow at the boys. "Going out?"

Red nodded. "We thought we might take a walk. Bob has never really had a chance to study Jupiter properly."

"All right," she agreed. "Don't be too late."

The people here acted as if the day and night they lived by were real, Bob had discovered. The twenty-four hour period of Earth made the colony's nights and days, probably because the body was adjusted for such intervals in its sleeping cycle. But it was hard to tell the real day and night apart, except for the color of the light. He glanced up at Jupiter, which seemed to fill a huge part of the sky directly overhead.

"She said they came from there," he remembered.

Red nodded. "I don't think she knows much more than we do—but she had to get those trinkets from somewhere. I want to know where."

They turned north, into the rougher country, beyond the colony. Red set a stiff pace, and Bob found it hard to keep up. The light from Jupiter seemed to come from all directions, yet the absence of air here prevented diffusion. He started to speak, but Red shook his head, pointing to the radio. Naturally, Penny could pick up anything they said over that. Bob cut his off. They could communicate safely by touching helmets when they needed to.

He found he was sweating and hot inside the suit, and his muscles were still tired from the work of the afternoon. But he continued on. Now they turned down a gulley, losing sight of the village. There was a scattering of fine dirt and small pebbles here, and Red bent over.

Bob touched helmets with him, and heard the other's satisfied grunt. "See? There's a footprint, and it's about her size. She's heading this way, all right. And I'll bet I know where she goes. Come on."

He began trotting forward, and Bob felt his chest heaving as he tried to keep up. He wasn't yet used to running in one of these suits. Apparently Red realized it, and slowed again.

They came to the top of a small rise in the gulley floor and looked down. Red muttered something and scrambled up a big rock, holding his hand for Bob to follow.

Far ahead, a little figure was trudging alone, carrying what seemed to be a bag. She wasn't looking around but heading straight toward a cleft between two huge rocks ahead. Once she stopped, seemed to cover her footprints, then went on.

"She probably remembers that trick about half the time," Red said. "I'll bet she misses more than she covers. But you can see she's trying to sneak off without being followed."

He took what Bob guessed must be a short cut. The ground was rougher than the trail Penny was following, and he still had trouble keeping up, but this route seemed to shorten the distance from Penny. At the top of another rise, they spotted her again, and she seemed to be nearer. But now she was hurrying, no longer making any effort to hide her tracks.

Now Bob forced his aching legs into the best trot he could manage. It wasn't too bad, once he got the hang of it. The inertia of his suit body tended to smooth out his speed, if he handled it just right.

Red caught him a few minutes later and touched helmets. "Better take it easy from now on. She'll hear our steps through the ground if we keep on like this."

They slowed, while Bob's chest rose and fell. He reached out to adjust his oxygen valve, and the richer mixture seemed to help somewhat. But he couldn't risk too much of that for fear of oxygen intoxication. As soon as his breathing seemed to quiet down, he cut the valve back.

Now there seemed to be a faint glow ahead, and Penny appeared at the edge of a cut in the rocks. She began moving downward. They were within a quarter mile of her. A few minutes later, they came to the same cut where she had been.

There was a glow, but it was a reflection from the rocks, which bent in a crooked trail, cutting off any direct view of what lay below.

There was a faint thudding sound coming from under Bob's boots now, as if something near by was jarring the ground. It stopped almost at once, however.

Here the rocks were even thicker, and the trail narrowed. The faint glow came from rocks above them now. Bob wasn't even sure it was more than a trick of reflected light from Jupiter. They moved forward steadily, expecting to see Penny. Then they caught sight of her, just as she began to run. She was waving one arm, in which she carried the package. She couldn't be more than five hundred feet ahead.

They moved forward more carefully now, making sure that their feet did not disturb any of the big rocks.

Ahead, the rocks thinned out, and they were soon at the spot where Penny had started running. Before them lay a natural little hollow in the ground, almost circular. It was like a shallow crater, perhaps a mile across, with rounded edges. At one time, it might have been a crater produced by meteorite collision, but, if so, time had somehow smoothed out the outlines. A lot of plants were growing wild here, but all seemed to be what Kirby had called weeds.

Then they came around one pillar of stone into full view of the depression, and Bob gasped.

He'd been almost prepared for what he saw, but there was still a shock to the reality. Down there a few hundred feet was the globe ship that had attacked the *Procyon*—or one exactly like it. It was nothing but a great white sphere, three hundred feet in diameter, glowing faintly. There were no openings that he could see, but now three smaller globes projected from the bottom, seeming to serve as legs on which it rested.

Then as he looked there was a slight change. One area of the globe from space began to turn color. Patterns appeared on it, shifting and dancing like those in the bit of plastic from Penny's room. These were much simpler, however, consisting of only a few lines or colors. They danced about, then steadied. Now two lines appeared, without the colors, and began tracing out patterns, changing angles, alternately drawing closer together and farther apart.

Below them appeared pictures. They were weird scenes, as if distorted in a dozen different ways. But Bob began to make sense of one. It was clearly the *Procyon*, false in colors and badly foreshortened, but still recognizable. It faded almost at once, to give place to another scene.

This took longer to recognize, until a spot of bright color seemed to appear behind it, flickering gently. It was obvious now—the rough picture of a regular rocket ship, with flame roaring out of its motors.

He was creeping closer, torn between fear and curiosity, when he saw Penny. She had come up almost under the ship and was looking at the glowing panel. Now she reached up to another section of the hull. Her hands seemed to disappear against the vastness of the ship, but as he drew closer he could see that she was tracing patterns, using her two arms to draw the lines that now began to appear on the glowing section. As her arms moved, tracing lines, the hull reproduced them above her.

A moment later, she stepped back, while new patterns

appeared on the side of the hull. She made a gesture of some kind as the last pattern was repeated. Then she nodded and began moving forward.

A small section of the hull opened—one large enough to have swallowed a man, though seeming nothing but a dot against the huge sphere. Penny picked up her bag and began to move toward the opening.

Red was up with a leap, crashing down the sides of the depression. He was apparently shouting, since his mouth was moving, but his radio was still off and no sound reached the girl. She was almost beside the opening now.

Bob stopped his own headlong rushing to flip on his radio. "Penny! Penny, stop! Don't go in there!"

She swung about quickly. Bob was rushing forward now. His mind was full of pictures of the globe attacking the *Procyon* and casually ripping away the bubble, but his fear didn't matter. He had to reach the other side of the girl before she could try to get away from Red and head toward the opening.

Then Red had her. She hadn't tried to avoid him. Bob slowed himself, glancing up at the ship that loomed far above his head.

There were no glowing panels now. The little opening had snapped closed. As silently and effortlessly as a shadow rising, the huge bulk began to lift. The three lower spheres disappeared into the hull, and the globe moved upwards. Suddenly it picked up speed, accelerating at a seemingly impossible rate, and dwindled into the distance toward Jupiter.

8 / Alien Contact

PENNY WAS CRYING FURIOUSLY when Red snapped on her radio. She began screaming at him, until he snapped it off again and held the switch down. Finally she began to quiet down, and he released her.

"Now you've done it," she complained. "You've scared them off, and I couldn't even exchange presents. You're both mean, bad boys, and I don't like you any more at all."

"You're not a very nice girl either," Red told her. "Your mother would be going crazy if she knew——"

"But she doesn't. She never knows!"

"It doesn't matter. She'd know you were gone if you walked into that ship and they closed the door and took you away!"

Abruptly she laughed. "Pooh! I've been in there dozens of times. It's awful cold there and dark, but that's where they put the presents for me. I give them what they like, and they give me all kinds of nice things. They wouldn't steal me."

Bob was beginning to suspect she was right and that he had been needlessly frightened at seeing her move toward the opening. There must have been plenty of other contacts, if she could communicate with them. And she had received other baubles safely.

"How long has this been going on, Penny?" he asked.

"Why should I tell you?" she wanted to know. She frowned at him uncertainly. "I liked you, Bob Wilson. I was even going to let you meet them. I was just going to tell them about how I'd bring you the next time. And then you betray me. Don't deny it, you betrayed me. And now I don't like you any more."

He grinned, but managed to keep her from seeing it. "That's all right, then, Penny. I don't care whether you like me or not any more, since you won't answer simple questions."

She thought that over, and finally nodded. "All right. I've been coming here for about four years. Ever since they saved me the first time I ran away and got lost."

"She did run away and get lost four years ago," Red said. He puzzled it over. "She was gone for three days while we sent out search parties. Then she appeared half a mile from the colony, up in the west hills, where we'd already looked a dozen times."

"That's right," she agreed. "I was lost and hungry and I felt terrible. That's when they found me. I was a long ways away, but I wasn't afraid any more when they came down. They made pictures, and I told them I was lost in every way I could. They opened that little door and I climbed in, and they took me back where I could see my home. And they showed more pictures inside the door, so I could find them again."

"You promised you'd never run away again," Red began.

She shook her head. "I didn't. Going to see friends isn't running away."

Bob was remembering some of the theories of speech he'd learned. Children could learn new languages because they hadn't learned to think in fixed patterns. After they had used any one language long enough, they began to think within the limits of that language and couldn't move beyond those limits.

"How do you talk with them?" he asked.

Penny frowned. "We don't talk. We—we. . . . There's no word. It's like growing in. They don't use words. Just the way the words make you see how things go."

Red started to laugh, but Bob cut it off. "I think I know what she means, Red. They don't have symbols for things and grammar to show how the things operate on each other. They use some kind of symbol for the relationship. It's like calculus instead of arithmetic. We use a language that piles ones on top of ones in tight bits of information, while they use a speech that shows the pattern all the bits add up to. There have been proposals for such languages, but nobody could ever design one that would work."

Penny thought it over. "I guess maybe you understand," she decided. "And maybe I like you again. But you shouldn't have scared them."

"They didn't get scared so easily when they attacked the *Procyon*," Red told her. "They were brave enough then—and they didn't care what happened to us."

She sighed. "I told them they were bad, and they said they were sorry. But they didn't know it was a—a people ship. It was going the wrong way, and it didn't look like any people ship they ever saw. It had something on it people don't use, too. They had to crack that off to get what they needed inside. But they won't do it again. They promised."

"All right, Penny," Red decided. "We'll talk about it later. Right now, we'd better head for home."

He picked her up and put her on his shoulder as easily as if he hadn't been running miles to catch her. Bob winced at the idea of carrying such a load, glad that it wasn't expected of him. One of Red's hands came up to cut her radio switch, and she made no effort to stop it.

"She can probably hear me through her suit," Red said quietly. "But it will be blurred. What do you think of her story? Is she a pet—or a trained spy?"

Bob couldn't decide. He hadn't thought of the pet idea, but it wasn't too impossible. Men on Earth sometimes caught other animals and played with them. A man would go to ridiculous extremes to get a puppy and care for it. Maybe to aliens, a child might be a similar pet. Or there might be a more sinister intent.

"They seem to know something of human ships," he admitted. "Those pictures of the two ships fitted what she was saying—they were showing why they didn't think the *Procyon* was one of her ships. But they've made no effort to contact us. Instead, they find a child and begin bribing her and teaching her their sign language. What better way to find out all about us without risking anything until they're ready to strike?"

"That's about how I see it," Red agreed. "And they must have some wonderful weapons if they can crack the protective field off that way. I suppose the lead she brings is useful, too. On a world of low density with mostly gaseous territory, like Jupiter, heavy metal must be rarer than radium used to be on Earth. I suppose it was the uranium in the bubble they wanted."

Bob let the conversation drop. He knew he should be thinking of what they would have to report to the colony, but he seemed to be having difficulty focusing his mind. The long hike, on top of the hard day, had been too much for him, obviously. His muscles ached. Even his neck ached. He could feel sweat trickling across his skin, and the temperature regulator in the suit seemed to be out of order.

Red stopped to rest, and Bob sank down with a sign of relief. He'd begun to think that the other boy was made of solid steel. Penny must have been asleep, since she stirred now and reached for her radio switch.

"They're nice," she said. Her voice was thick, as if she were still not fully awake.

"Sure," Bob agreed. "What are they like, Penny? How do they look?"

"I dunno. I never saw them. They can't live out here where it's so thin. But they're nicer than anyone. And I like their presents."

There wasn't much argument that could be presented in answer to that. It began to sound as if they really must be from Jupiter, since anyone from inside that planetary atmosphere wouldn't be able to live—except under enormous pressure—where it was presumably thick.

Red got up with the girl again, moving her to his other shoulder. He watched as Bob staggered clumsily to his feet. "You okay, Bob?"

"Sure," Bob told him. "Only I'm so dead tired I can hardly stand up or keep my eyes open."

"I should have remembered you're not used to moving very far in one of those things. Sorry. We'll be home pretty soon now."

Mercifully, Red took a slower speed the rest of the way. But even that was too much for Bob. When the colony was in sight, he found his legs almost collapsing. He called a halt and dropped to the ground. His lungs were laboring again, and the heat regulator in the suit was in worse condition. He'd have to get it fixed when he got back.

To make things worse, the bad condition of his air was giving him a headache. He struggled to his feet and clumped along behind Red, but every step hurt. There was a hammer in his skull that seemed to strike with each movement of his legs.

He turned the oxygen valve up again, and it seemed to help. The growing thickness cleared from his brain, and he moved more easily, though the headache didn't get better.

Then he saw that there was a house just ahead of him, and he took new hope from that. They'd be at home soon, and he could find something to cure the headache, at least. A good night's sleep would fix him up. And maybe he wouldn't go to Kirby's farm tomorrow. He needed a rest. Maybe he'd just sleep instead. . . .

"Bob! Hey, Bob, wake up!"

He was conscious of someone shouting at him, and woke to see Red thumping against the front of his suit. Penny was on the ground, staring around in a semi-conscious state.

Apparently he'd dozed off in his suit. He couldn't understand why he hadn't fallen until he realized they were on the main street of the colony and he was leaning against an entrance. Then he saw that the entrance was the McCarthys' and that he was blocking the seal.

He moved groggily aside, and the headache began pounding again. Red looked at him strangely, but said nothing more until they were inside. Then he began trying to take his suit off. He had to get the helmet off and get some decent air!

They must have made a fair amount of noise, he realized as the helmet snapped back. Mrs. McCarthy was standing in the door of the parlor, clutching a dressing gown around her.

"Why Red! You didn't say you were taking Penny with you. And staying out to this hour!" She made clucking sounds with her tongue and began leading her daughter away. "Penny, you get right out of that suit and into your pajamas immediately! The idea, staying out this late with those boys!"

They moved off toward the sleeping level, just as McCarthy came up. His eyes were red, and he looked groggy, but he took in their suits at a glance, and his eyes moved to Red. At the expression he saw on his nephew's face, he motioned toward the office.

Bob managed to get out of his suit somehow. The air still seemed thick and too warm to him, but he supposed that was just his own built-up body heat from the steaming temperature of the suit. He spotted a bottle of aspirin and slipped two out and onto his tongue while Red struggled with a twisted strap. But for the moment, he was feeling better, even without the medicine.

McCarthy came in, carrying a jug of steaming coffee and three cups. He poured for all of them. "What's up? More trouble tonight?"

Bob drank the coffee gratefully, and again felt a lift. He went on sipping, letting Red tell the story. But Red seemed reluctant. "What trouble, Uncle Frank? We've been out of the colony. Something serious?"

"It's serious enough, I'm afraid." McCarthy stared thoughtfully at Bob, frowned, and then turned back to his coffee. He sighed. "We had our first two cases of plague tonight. Or it looks like the plague. The two young Lemonn brothers."

"Are you sure?" Bob asked.

"No—but it seems to be. I checked by radio with Earth. Reception is terrible when we have to relay through the automatic station on Callisto, but what I got of the reply seems to give the same symptoms. It's something like a disease we've had here for years, but never this bad. I just got back half an hour ago, and I've been expecting more emergency calls ever since. What's the matter with you, Bob?"

It had begun to hit him again, Bob realized. Apparently just reaching home had given him a temporary lift, but now the sick fatigue was creeping back. The headache wasn't quite as bad, but the room seemed stifling, and the air seemed bad.

"He's bushed," Red said. "He worked all afternoon with Kirby, which is enough to kill a horse. Then I led him on a forced march up to the Bowl and back, and he's not used to all that in a suit."

McCarthy nodded. "Better get to bed, then. And stop trying to do everything at once. Now, what did you have to tell me, Red?"

"Penny ran off again, and——"

"She couldn't have. I locked her room myself," McCarthy protested.

"Well, she unlocked it, then. Almost any key will work on that door, and she's no fool. She's been running out every time Ganymede is between Jupiter and the sun for the past four years."

"I suppose so." The doctor sighed again, refilling his cup. "I've caught her slipping out a few times, but she won't stop. I thought maybe the lock would help. You know how her mother is. She spoils the child, but I suppose I do, too. Anyhow, she always comes back from whatever nonsense she goes out for, and there's nothing here to hurt her."

Bob realized that the doctor was almost as tired as he was and that he was saying things that only half fitted with what he meant. The boy nodded heavily. That's the way it was, he decided. Nothing meant anything anyway, and language should slip, not bunch all up together. . . .

"You'd better get to bed if you're that tired," the doctor told him sharply. "You're almost falling off the chair. Red, can't all this wait until morning when we've had some sleep?"

"I suppose so. I guess it will have to," Red decided. "Sorry I woke you up, Uncle Frank."

The doctor muttered something, shaking his head. He reached for the coffee again, then pushed it aside and turned toward the stairs that led down to the bedrooms. Bob stood up groggily to follow. He felt Red's arm around him and leaned gratefully against the other. More stumbling than walking, he got down the stairs and into his own room.

"I'll be all right now—" he started to say.

Then it hit him fully. The room seemed like a blast furnace. He couldn't breathe. And his legs were too weak to hold him. He took two staggering steps toward the bed before he lost control. He saw the floor coming up at him, put out a hand, and barely saved himself from cracking his nose.

Red bent over to help him up. Then the other boy's hand was against his forehead.

Red was out of the room at once, shouting. "Uncle Frank! Uncle Frank!"

Funny, Bob thought. He put his own hand to his forehead and felt sweat there. His hand felt hot. Then his forehead felt even hotter.

He was only half conscious as Red and McCarthy rushed in and began lifting him to the bed. The doctor was calling himself names bitterly.

"Right under my nose. Red, if this had been anyone but in my own family, I'd have seen it at once. But no, I have to sit talking nonsense while Bob almost passes out. It's the old story. A doctor is not without competence, save in his own household. Here, help me get this shirt off him."

" 'Sall right. You're tired too," Bob muttered. "Be all right. Just need sleep. . . ."

If they'd only let him alone! But they wouldn't. He felt McCarthy probing and prying.

"Do you have a headache?" the doctor asked. "Here— and here?"

Bob nodded. The motion sent fresh lances of pain

through him. Something was thrust into his mouth and under his tongue. That finally registered. They thought he was sick. And he never was sick!

He must have muttered the thought aloud as the thermometer was removed. "You're sick now, Bob," McCarthy said. "Very sick. You've got a temperature of a hundred and four right now, and you should be more delirious than you are."

From somewhere inside himself, Bob found one tiny bit of strength. He clung to it, getting ready to use it. Then he thrust himself up on his arms and faced the doctor. He had trouble focusing his eyes, but he forced the one moment of clarity into his head.

"Dr. McCarthy, is it the plague? Is that what's wrong with me?"

McCarthy nodded. "It's the plague, Bob. The same symptoms. Now stop fighting against it and relax. If you don't, I'll have to give you something to knock you out."

He let the doctor push him back. Then he relaxed. Waves of blackness swept over him. He was in a hot, black oven. He sank farther into it, until he was unconscious.

9 / Sick Bay

THERE WAS A LONG period of confusion in which he could be sure only that he was hot and felt terrible. Sometimes he heard himself babbling words that he knew made no sense. At other times he thought he was being terribly rational, only to come to with the realization that he had been delirious.

He came to full consciousness finally in a darkened room. It wasn't his bedroom, he was sure. Then he realized that it was the same room, but that an extra bed had been brought in. A man lay there, gasping weakly, and he recognized that the man was George Lemonn, one of the farmers. The man looked terrible. His face was red, and there were small yellow spots all over it. He shouldn't be breathing that way.

He saw a woman in a white dress at the door and motioned for her. She was beside him at once, reaching for a thermometer. But he shook it aside. "You'd better look after him," he said, pointing to Lemonn. "I think he's sick."

"We'll take care of him," the woman said. He saw with surprise that it was Mrs. McCarthy. But she didn't act as he remembered her. She seemed efficient and very sure of herself, which was something that had never been true of Mrs. McCarthy's manner. And she wasn't offering him anything to eat. He looked again, and she smiled. "It's still me, Bob. I used to be a very good nurse, a long time ago, and I guess I can still remember how."

He nodded, too weak to be greatly surprised. "I've been sick, too, I guess. What day is it?"

"The ninth."

It shocked him. He'd been sure that weeks had passed, but it had been only two days. "Am I all over it now?"

She smiled again, and there was the total assurance of mercy itself in her voice. "Of course, you're going to be all right, Bob. You just rest until the doctor comes back."

He'd been to visit one of his friends in a hospital often enough to know how to read what nurses said. Her words meant that he was still sick and she didn't know what would happen. If he'd really been well, she would have laughed at him. And if he'd been going to get worse, she'd have been twice as sweet about it.

"Where's the other Lemonn?"

"Shh." She shook her head and reached for the thermometer. This time he let her insert it under his tongue. So Roger Lemonn had died. The plague really could kill!

She got up to move aside as Dr. McCarthy came in. The doctor took the thermometer and studied it. "Good morning, Bob," he said. "Your temperature is down almost to normal this morning."

"It won't stay down unless somebody tells me the truth," Bob told him.

McCarthy smiled tiredly and dropped onto the edge of

the bed. "Most patients don't mean that," he said. "But I think you do. All right, I don't know what to tell you. You've gotten through one very serious crisis a lot faster than I thought you would. But you're a sick boy still, and you'll probably have other attacks. What happens then I don't know, but my guess is that you'll pull through."

"How many people?" Bob asked.

"Four so far—the two Lemonns, you, and a prospector you never met, who just came in yesterday. He seems to have a milder case. If it gets any worse, we're going to clear out one of the processing sheds and turn it into a hospital." He stood up then. "Now, do you feel better?"

"Not much," Bob admitted. "How am I supposed to feel when I may have spread this thing in the first place?"

The doctor shook his head. "If that's all that worries you, Bob, forget it. This is a Gany disease. It's too much like one that I've seen often enough before, but grown a lot more dangerous. It's some pestilence we've developed right here. The *Procyon* must have picked it up here, too. Though I can't figure why they came down so quickly when it took us until now to develop it."

He moved off, and now Bob did feel better. The headache was gone, and he could feel no signs of fever. He was weak, as he found when he tried to move his hands, but otherwise he wasn't too uncomfortable.

He lay there, trying to remember everything he had ever read in his father's books or heard from his father's friends. There were bits about the vector of a disease, but he kept getting that vector mixed up with mathematical vector analysis, when the two had almost nothing to do with each other.

104

He realized he was going to sleep and stopped fighting against it.

When he came to, he was shaking violently and his whole body seemed frozen. Now there were a few yellow spots on his hands. He forced his teeth to stop chattering and managed to look around. He was in another place. They'd moved him while he was asleep, and this was a single large room, with each bed separated from the others by a curtain held up by ropes.

Maria Sanchez came through the curtain, saw he was awake, and came closer. She was smiling uncertainly. This was certainly no professional nurse.

"Do they all get the shakes?" he asked. It was hard to get the words out.

"Yes, Bob. And then the fever very quickly again. Dr. McCarthy said I was to tell you the truth, so I guess it's all right."

He forced a smile to his lips, unable to speak again. She tried to smile back and then went quietly away.

The fever seemed to follow the tremors with almost no break. One minute he was freezing, and the next he was roasting. But he had expected it this time, and it wasn't so bad. The headache was there again, but by lying very still, he could avoid the worst of the pain. The fever mounted, and then he lost rationality.

This time Kirby was sitting beside him when he came to. He was weaker than before, unable to get his hands up to find the glass of water. The old man helped him, holding his head up gently. A faint smile came onto the old lips.

"They thought Davy Dreadnaught was sick once. It was

right after he filled up all the Martian canals, and all that red dust made him look feverish. So they clapped him in sick bay. Well, you can guess that made him mad. He got hotter and hotter. And the hotter under the collar he got, the more sick they thought he was. And that made him hotter still."

It was a very long and rambling story this time, and Bob lost the point of it sometime after Davy Dreadnaught escaped and got to Venus, still so hot that when he bathed in the ocean there, it all turned to steam and created the clouds on the planet. He drifted off to sleep while Kirby's voice went droning quietly on.

He knew somehow that he was going to be all right, and he slept peacefully, to waken with only the weakness bothering him. His father was there this time.

"I've just seen a blood sample, and you're all right," Dr. Wilson said. His face showed more strain than when he'd had the stroke, but now he was smiling. "We'll get you home as soon as you can stand up long enough for us to put a suit on you."

That was the hardest day of all. To know he was over the plague and still had to be tended to like a baby threatened to break his temper a dozen times. Maybe that was why they finally released him before they had promised. He needed help at first, and his legs were shaky, but he managed to walk back to the McCarthys' house and find his way to the couch in the parlor.

McCarthy watched him with genuine satisfaction. "You're doing splendidly. You should be just going through the second stage, with the critical period coming up. But every sign says you're over it. You're lucky, Bob. Your body is one of those that seems to make antibodies in large quantities and in a hurry. Right now your blood must be loaded with an antibody against this plague. No wonder you never were seriously sick before. I wish others were more like that."

"Are there many more?" Bob had only a dim memory of the hospital, but he was sure it wasn't filled yet.

"Only two more. George Lemonn seems to be going to recover, but I don't think one of the new cases will. But so far, it isn't as bad as it might be. We've found something that helps, at least. Massive doses of vitamin C!"

He sounded bitter, and Bob realized he had a right to be. The vitamin supply had been lost on the *Procyon*. The ship had looted its own stores to make up as much as it could, but it had been only a small amount of what was to have been supplied originally.

It was probably the stripping of the ship stores that had caused the plague on the way back to Earth, Bob learned. Or so McCarthy and Wilson had decided. The ship must have cut itself down to less than normal dosage, figuring that they could risk it, since they would soon be back on Earth.

In the meantime, of course, they'd picked up whatever caused the plague. Apparently, this whole moon was now infected, and some of the disease-causing organisms must have been carried into the ship. There, working on people who had never developed any immunity to it, and with bodies already low on vitamin C, it had developed into a full epidemic before the first true case had matured here.

"Then they might save most of the people on the ship?" Bob asked.

McCarthy reached for the coffee, sipping it as he considered. "I sent a radio message giving them all the information I had, of course," he said. "I haven't received any reply. But it's such a simple treatment that somebody must have decided to send up a supply of the vitamin to the ship. How much good it will do depends on how bad the cases are. It should save some of them, at least. But it's not really a cure, Bob. We haven't found that yet, though your body managed it. We need some way to get antibodies."

"I've already volunteered a pint of your blood when you can safely give it," Wilson told his son. "I knew you'd agree."

There could be no argument about that. Bob knew that all he could give wouldn't be enough to help many people. But it would serve another purpose. With it, Dr. Wilson could begin a full study of both the cause of the infection and the antibody. So far, they weren't sure of what organism here caused it, but the antibody would be specifically designed by Bob's system to neutralize that one type of cell, and whatever reacted with the antibody would have to be the thing they were looking for.

It was still all speculation. So far they had no real proof that the plague was caused by any life form native to Ganymede—they had only McCarthy's guess for that. They didn't know how vitamin C helped, nor could they tell why the disease had broken out so suddenly.

"It acts like an old and very minor disease that has suddenly gone through some radical change," Wilson said. "We've had plenty of those on Earth. There have been long periods when influenza was only a mild infection. Then something happens, and it turns virulent. When that happens, it kills millions—or it used to, before we learned to handle it. It will even reinfect people who are supposedly made immune by previous exposure to the old form. That must have happened here."

Bob shivered as he remembered the words of farmer Kirby. When some form of life was made available in large quantities, there would be some plague around to discover it and make the most of it. Kirby had been referring to plant pests, but it could apply just as well to people.

"In that case, does it mean all those who should be immune can still get it?" he asked.

McCarthy nodded. "Not only can, Bob, but do! If I'm right about what disease this was before, both the Lemonns had already had it. But they were the first to come down with this. For all we know, everyone may come down with it here next week—or sooner."

"Maybe you'd better take that blood sample right now," Bob suggested. "The sooner you begin work on that, the better off we'll be."

McCarthy looked doubtful. At last he stood up and went to get his equipment. "I hate doing this now," he said. "But you're right. And I guess a little won't weaken you. How about fifty cubic centimeters, Noel?"

"It won't be enough, but I can probably learn something with it," Wilson admitted. "All right, prepare it for me and I'll take it to the laboratory in the morning."

Bob hardly noticed the effect. He'd always been lucky enough to have no reaction to such things. He waited until McCarthy prepared the sample and gave it to his father. Then he considered what else he could do. He wasn't trained for biochemical or medical research, unfortunately. But he'd done a lot of work for his father in tracing down organisms by mathematical analysis.

"Do you have complete notes of your cases for the last five years, Dr. McCarthy?" he asked.

"For the last twenty. I never threw them away."

He found one of the cards. At this stage there was no use trying to maintain secrecy as to the name of the patient. It was far more important to find some way to help other patients. Bob looked over the neatly arranged notes. There should be enough information for at least a tentative conclusion.

"I can put this through the computer after I break it down, and see what kind of a pattern develops," he suggested. "I might even be able to prove whether it's one of these diseases you've listed. Would that help?"

"I'll have your computer moved up to the back of my office where you can get to my files easily," McCarthy told him. "Better get to bed, Bob, if you're going to try anything in the morning."

Bob started to protest that he'd already had too much sleep, but he caught himself yawning. It seemed impossible that he could be sleepy again, but he was.

He was just starting toward his room when there was a pounding on the entrance. McCarthy went to answer it and came back with the grimness on his face again. He picked up his equipment.

"Two more cases of the plague," he reported. "At this rate, we'll be out of vitamin C in a few more days."

He went out hurriedly.

10 / Quarantine

BOB WOKE UP RAVENOUSLY hungry but feeling almost normal. His legs seemed firm under him, and he dressed without any sign of weakness. He found that nearly everyone was gone, leaving only Red. There was breakfast still warm in the oven, however, and he wolfed it down.

"Did you tell your uncle about Penny?" Bob asked.

Red hesitated for a moment. "No," he admitted. "With all this, I didn't figure it was worth worrying people more than they are right now. Besides, I'm not so sure now that we had the whole business figured out right."

"I'm not quite sure what we decided," Bob admitted. "It's all blurred. Did they get things set up for me to go to work?" At Red's nod, he began hurrying through his breakfast. "Umm. We didn't figure that the globe ship might have planted the plague here to weaken us, did we?"

Red frowned, obviously not liking the idea. "I don't see it. How could they know what would hit us, unless they know a lot more about our make-up than they seem to?"

It was a good question, and Bob had no answer. He finished his breakfast as Red made ready to go to the laboratory.

Then he headed for the doctor's office. There was a small room in back where most of the files were, and the computer had been moved in and was waiting there.

It had seemed simpler last night, however, than it was when looked at in the cold light of day. He had to break down all the careful notes and take out those elements which were significant and capable of being programmed. Only after that was done, and each card marked for its significant values, could he use the computer.

He heard a sound from the entrance and went out, expecting another call for McCarthy. But it was Dan Kirby. The old man came in, studying Bob.

"Just a social call to see how you're doing," he said. "But I guess from the looks of you that you're doing fine." He followed Bob back to the little office, watching as Bob puzzled over his problem. "Or maybe you're not doing so well. Anything I can do?"

Bob couldn't see how. This work would require someone trained in indexing and sorting. He really needed a card punch and sorter. But he tried to explain his problem, as much to clarify it for himself as to satisfy Kirby's curiosity. This morning, he'd have been glad not to see the old man, though he remembered with gratitude the long vigil beside his bed at the hospital.

Kirby took off his coat and picked up a pencil. "Maybe I can do a better job than you figure," he said. "I got trained to be an accountant before I ran away to space, and I held just about every kind of job there. Suppose we list all the factors we can, and then we both can start indexing these cards."

The old man's eyes were still sharp enough to scan a card

and catch every detail at first glance, and he made his notes in a fine copperplate hand that was as clear as printing. He also seemed to have an excellent memory for everything they discussed.

"You wouldn't know how to run a computer, would you?" Bob asked him.

"Nope. Never got further than regular desk calculators and bookkeeping machines. I wanted to go for a home-study course in higher mathematics and cybernetics once, but then I got out here, and the mail is too slow. But I did learn how to work. Takes the first fifty years of a man's life to do that. So you punch the machine and leave this to me."

Even with Kirby doing most of the routine work, it was slow going. Most of the information being handled would be useless—the inevitable noise, or redundancy, found in notes not especially made for analysis. And until he had gone through a good bit of preliminary trial, Bob couldn't be sure what factors should be used. A top-flight programmer could probably have done it all much faster, but he stuck to methods he knew to be within his grasp.

At noon Kirby got up and went for the kitchen.

"Bring me a sandwich too," Bob called out.

The old man snorted. "Sandwich! I'm fixing to cook a meal. With everyone in this family working on the plague, I figured I'd be more useful taking care of things than farming right now. I wanted to see you, sure—but somebody has to do rough work at a time like this."

Something began to smell good. Bob heard dark mutterings about the way women kept things hidden, but Kirby seemed to find them. When Mrs. McCarthy came rushing in, the food was just coming off the stove. She stared in shocked surprise, darting for the kitchen. Then she relaxed and even smiled. "I must say you keep the kitchen neat, Dan," she admitted.

"Had to learn that in a ship's galley," he told her.

Kirby's cooking wasn't as good as Mrs. McCarthy's, Bob realized. But it was a lot better than could be found in most homes. Red and Wilson came in and ate quickly. McCarthy was still at the hospital, and Kirby packed a lunch for him. Mrs. McCarthy took it to him when she left with the others. Kirby gathered up the dishes and began washing them. He was back in the office shortly.

"Worked as a houseboy for the governor of Mars one season," he said. "That was during the Martian fever. I never fancied the job, but someone had to do it. Wish we had some information on file for the years before the doctor came. Most of my troubles came earlier. I'd like to find out what I had, now."

"How are the people taking it?" Bob asked.

Kirby drew out a pipe and stuffed it, taking his time about answering. "They're beginning to simmer, but they haven't boiled over yet. They don't really believe it's happening. I hear that everything is going to be all right as soon as the supply rocket reaches us from Earth. That must be about due, since they sent it out on top acceleration. And they figure some of those laboratories on Earth will find a cure, anyhow. But still, maybe they're tougher than I think. Maybe they can take it when they get all the bad news. I hope so. Hey—Doc made a mistake here." He made a careful note. "Mrs. Henny was sick right after her second baby—

114

that's in '85, not '84. Guess he hadn't switched over yet so soon after New Year's."

Bob looked and decided it wasn't that important. Besides, Kirby was probably right.

By the end of the day, there were enough cards indexed for Bob to begin running them through the machine. It was a lot faster than the other operation. And now it began to make sense. Some of the data they had was obviously useless, and the cards would have to be gone over again for still other information. But a general pattern began to appear as the machine ground out its results.

McCarthy came in finally. He was going to need hospitalization himself, Bob decided. There was a limit to what one man could take. And at least half his work was due to calls that were false alarms. When anyone had a headache now, there was a wild emergency call. But he seemed to be more grim than tired. He watched Kirby getting dinner without comment. Finally he seemed to realize what was going on. "Thanks, Dan," he called. "Got any coffee?"

He sat sipping it until the others came in. The table was set by then, and Bob stopped his work to join them.

"There's a general meeting of the colony," McCarthy announced. "Sanchez is calling it, probably to avoid having people take the authority into their own hands. We'd all better show up."

"News from Earth?" Red guessed.

McCarthy nodded. "Naturally. And of course our town crier, Larry Coccagna, had to spread it at once. Why Sanchez lets him near the radio I'll never figure out." He grimaced. "Earth has declared Ganymede colony a plague area and quarantined us until after the danger is over. That means we're cut off from the rest of the system unless we can whip this. They're scared."

"But what about medical help? Supplies? Maybe some doctors from Mars?" Bob asked.

"Taboo now. We're on our own, except for what can be sent by unmanned ship."

"Won't make any difference," Kirby said. "That's all we could get in time to help, anyhow. But it's going to worry most folks." He snorted. "And make a few mad, which may be a good thing."

Bob found himself in the group that was mad, as they moved toward the big plant processing shed where all could meet. At the moment, if he had had a means to be transported instantly back to Earth with his father and to the finest university there, he'd have refused. He was ashamed of his home planet for what they were doing to these people.

Sanchez was unhappy, but the Mayor was still running things. He found McCarthy's group and led them up to the front. "We want you to report what you know," he said. "They gotta listen to a doctor now."

There were demands that he read the telegram, and Sanchez rose. His voice carried over the mutterings, quieting them. The message was no different in content from what the doctor had reported, but it stirred the anger in Bob to fresh heights. It was a rotten gesture to make to people in trouble!

Apparently the people themselves thought so. There were shouts and screams.

"We gotta do something!" someone roared from the

116

back. "We gotta do something quick! Sanchez, we want a vote!"

Sanchez roared back. "We gotta act like human beings, not like animals. First we gotta find what we're up against. Doc, you tell them."

McCarthy tried, but there wasn't enough to tell. All he could do was repeat that they were already doing all they could and that Dr. Wilson and his son were busy with research on the problem.

The same voice shouted again: "Earth bums! We don't need no bums from Earth. They brought the stuff here from Titan, now they want to run us. Earth spies! We gotta do something. I vote we lynch the Earth spies!"

There were shocked voices at that, but there were also cries of assent. Bob felt the hair prickle on the back of his neck. He had never seen mob fury building up before. Lynchings had been gone from the scene on Earth for a century. But now he saw the group around the big man in the back begin to panic with him. A loud voice was all they needed, it seemed.

Dan Kirby got up quietly and slipped to the back while Sanchez was shouting for order. There was a brief scuffle, and then the old man was leading Hugh Tompkins forward, dragging the big man by the scruff of his neck and one ear. Kirby pitched him up onto the platform and sprang up beside him. His voice suddenly rang out in the hush of surprise.

"Folks, I want you to see a real live coward! A man who gets scared and so stupid with fear all he can think of is to kill somebody whose only crime has been trying to save him.

I've seen a lot like him, back on Mars during the fever. But most of you never saw a real coward. We don't have many out here. So take a good look. Hugh, take a bow to your audience! A deep bow. And then get out!"

"He'll never get away with it," Bob's father said softly.

Bob wasn't so sure. There was no logic in Kirby's action, but there had been no logic in Tompkins' cries, either. And then from somewhere, there was a laugh. It was nervous and uncertain, but it was the necessary spark. Others picked it up. As Kirby twisted his ear, Hugh Tompkins bowed again and then began trying to slip away. There were no more outcries against Dr. Wilson as the scientist stood up.

Bob expected some kind of technical report, and he hoped it could be made plain enough for the listeners. But Dr. Wilson went to the point more directly.

"The thing that is attacking you is something that gets in your blood and is too small to see with anything but an electron microscope. The best chance for a cure is something else that can be made in the blood of someone who recovers, and that is even smaller. Well, I have a sample of my son's blood and of every sick man's blood, and I've got the only electron microscope beyond Mars. I'm using it in the ways I've spent a lifetime learning to use it. And I think I'm beginning to get some results. I can't promise any miracles yet, but I think I'm somewhere on the track of the disease. I'd work hard on this problem for any group, because that's what I've been trained to do. But I'm going to try to work a little harder, because I've found I like it here among you! That's all I can say."

Kirby nodded emphatic approval. Bob heard a faint

spattering of applause, and then more. He should have known enough to trust his father, he decided. And he felt a sudden renewal of pride in him.

Sanchez looked down and motioned for Bob. "Bob, I hear you're working on this too. I dunno what you can get off a bunch of old records, but suppose you tell us?"

Bob felt uncomfortable on the platform. Then he let what he had learned speak for itself.

"I've found that Dr. McCarthy's guess was right. This is a disease that got started right here and has mutated recently. There is clear proof in the records. But I've also found something else more important. I've found that it isn't contagious. You don't have to worry about getting it from your friends or family. It's something we get from direct contact with some form of Ganymede life."

He stepped down quickly. There was less applause than there had been for his father, but he seemed to sense the tension in the big shed relaxing a little more. For some reason, contagious diseases were always more frightening than any others. When malaria was considered contagious, whole cities had panicked in blind fear; after it was proved to be caused by mosquitoes, just as many people in some towns died for a while, but there was an end to the panic.

Sanchez seemed to sense the relief and immediately dismissed the meeting. People began to move out, reluctantly at first, and then more steadily.

McCarthy pulled Bob aside. "Can you really prove that, Bob?" he asked.

"It's perfectly obvious. There is no period of spreading —no sign that one case follows another. The whole pattern

119

is typical of something contacted from the environment. Dad worked on a lot of odd diseases, and the patterns were always reliable for those that were contagious or non-contagious."

"Then we won't have to isolate cases, at least," the doctor decided. "That would be hard here, but I've been considering it. And if we can find the source, we might even prevent some of the cases. Anything more from the records?"

"Not yet—I've only had one day on them, and it may take a week to refine them down to a full pattern."

Sanchez came up then, wiping his face with a large kerchief. "That was close," he announced to McCarthy's little group. "I got all I want of that. Next time Larry spreads the news, I told him I'd shoot him. And I mean it, now. Good thing nobody thought too much about what you said, Bob."

Bob couldn't follow that, but Sanchez wasn't waiting to be asked. He mopped his head again, sighing.

"If Earth finds proof the stuff came from here and is something we got in our ground or whatever it is, how long you think before they drop the quarantine? They make it permanent! But we'll worry about that later, unless somebody thinks about it."

Bob felt his face stiffen and saw the same reaction on the faces of the others. Sanchez was right. If Earth discovered what Bob could prove, Ganymede would be permanently put out of bounds. And if anyone else thought of that, Tompkins might get his followers after all.

11 / Moon of Doom

NOBODY ELSE SEEMED TO realize the conclusions Sanchez had drawn. The plague wasn't speeding up yet, either. There were about two new cases a day. A couple of the victims recovered slowly, and this added a faint note of hope. But in the long run, the situation still looked hopeless. There was fear in all the eyes that Bob saw, and he suspected that the same emotion showed on his own face. He took to watching his father for signs.

Dr. Wilson seemed to be unaffected, however. He and Red were working long hours of overtime, trying to trace the cause of the disease. They had the blood from Bob, and a second pint had been taken from another patient and carefully hand-centrifuged to leave only the plasma which held the antibodies and could be stored.

With that and blood samples from the sick patients, Dr. Wilson had expected to find the problem fairly simple. But tracking down the dangerous Ganymede life form turned out to be difficult.

He showed Bob one of the slides through the microscope when Bob took time off to visit him. It seemed to be a perfect sample. There was evidence of some organism and proof that an antibody had blocked it.

"The only trouble is that it isn't the plague cause," Wilson explained bitterly. "Apparently everyone here has several dozen parasitical organisms native to this moon circulating in his blood. Most of them are only mildly harmful. You must have had most of them, too, since your blood had antibodies for all of them, as far as we can tell. One of the strains of parasites from the sick blood must be the cause of the plague. And one of the blood fractions we got from you must be the answer to it. But to try out every combination would take years."

"They trace things down on Earth," Bob objected.

"Certainly. They use experimental animals, such as rats or guinea pigs. They can run off a hundred at a time, if they have to, to find which is affected by what. But we don't have any animals on this whole moon, and we can't get any."

"Would this infect a rat, anyhow?" Red wondered aloud. "Dr. Wilson, maybe it only hits humans. I haven't heard of them trying it on animals on Earth."

"The news reports don't give enough details for us to know. I suppose it would work with almost any animal." Wilson considered it. "It should. After all, this evolved on a world where there was no Earth-adjusted life, but it has been able to infect us. That means it isn't as specialized as it may seem. There are a lot of diseases that will affect only one type of animal. But others, like gangrene, will infect any animal. And this adjusts to both Earth animal and Ganymede plant. You can't find anything much less selective than that."

Bob tried to find what hope there was of narrowing down

122

the research, but he could get no satisfactory reply. Apparently his father hadn't found any method yet.

He went back to work on his own research, but that had nearly reached a stalemate. The pattern now was more certain than before, but it offered no clues. He and Kirby had been over the reports, looking for any added factor, but they had already used everything that had any meaning.

He found McCarthy in the office, staring darkly at a nearly empty bottle. It had been full of pure ascorbic acid—or vitamin C—tablets once, but now there were only a few left.

"One dose for one patient," he said. "Which? And how do I keep the healthy people here from contracting the plague when this is gone?"

He scooped the few tablets out and into an envelope. Then he picked up his bag and prepared to go to the hospital. There had been four cases the day before. Any further increase would be more than some of the people could take without cracking—or so Sanchez thought.

Bob tried to think what else he could do. He should have every detail of the lives of the people here, probably. What they ate, what they wore, where they went, what they did—all might be factors that would show some other meaningful pattern.

Abruptly he pulled himself up and began climbing into his suit. There were other records—the work records for the processing plants and the crop records of the farmers. At that moment, he couldn't see how such material would help, but it was more data.

Sanchez raised no objections when he asked for the files.

"Take what you want, Bob. I don't care. We don't farm or work the plants much now, anyhow. Why? Who will buy what we produce? We have no market."

Bob hadn't thought of that angle of the quarantine. In the long run, it could be more serious than any other. A lot of people might die from the plague, but all would die if their supplies were permanently cut off.

Sanchez and his son Pete helped move the files to Dr. McCarthy's office. They took up most of the free space, but that hardly mattered, since McCarthy was spending most of his time at the improvised hospital. This time, Kirby was a better guide to the coding than Bob, since Kirby knew far more about the various things that could be done to the crops and the fermentation cultures.

When the work was ready for the computer there seemed to be a mountain of material. The new records had to be collated with the old, under the name of the person to whom it all applied. Bob finally was ready, however, and began feeding them into the computer.

The results were negative at first, but he'd expected that. The whole first day was disappointing. But toward noon of the second, he stopped, staring at what was pouring out on the tape of the machine.

"Mr. Kirby," he asked, "was that stuff we pulled the fungus off of called dumbspike?"

Kirby nodded. "Yep. It's got a sharp point on the stalk, so only a dumbbell would touch it. Or that's what they told me gave the plant its name." He got up and came over to the machine. Somehow in the course of their work, the old man had picked up enough of the machine code to understand most of it.

He ran the tape through his fingers. Then he nodded vigorously. "That's it! Has to be. And you're right. You worked with me on that—probably brought some in on your suit before you got sick. How tight does it check?"

"Seventy per cent," Bob answered. He ripped the finished tape free and began climbing into his suit. Considering the number of accidental encounters and false leads that must be mixed into the records, such a correlation was remarkably high.

Kirby joined him, but he was chewing on bitter thoughts. "We found that out just too late, Bob. Most of the dumbspike has been harvested and is being processed right now. Probably most people here have some traces of the stuff around their houses by now."

It was true. Bob could remember its being brought in. He had been interested in it as the first plant he'd ever helped to grow. Kirby was right: it was too late to isolate the source of the trouble for this season. But the information should still be useful.

Dr. Wilson studied the tape even more carefully than Kirby had. But there was almost a smile on his face as he handed it back. "I think that does it, Bob. We'll run a culture from some of the plants and the fungus you found. When we get that, we can compare it with the bugs found in the blood and test it with all the antibodies until we find the right one. That shouldn't take more than a day."

"Can we help?" Bob's project was finished now. He

knew there was no use trying to check on any more data, and there was no real work of any other kind for him.

"Get me some of the plant and fungus," his father suggested. "I'll begin preparing things here."

There was no trouble in getting a supply. Kirby found the plants still stacked near the processing shed. He hunted around among the rejects for some that had the smear of fungus on it and also took another specimen that looked clean. Then he and Bob sat down to watch as Wilson and Red began searching for the infective agent.

Luck, for once, was with them. There was one small cell that Wilson recognized at once. Even Bob could see that it was similar to one which had been found in the blood of sick patients. Red had made a pulp of some pieces of sterilized dumbspike, and the organism began growing rapidly on that, forming colonies that could be seen easily.

"Seems to be a decay bacterium," Wilson told Bob. "Harmless in the sap of the plant, but it breaks down any dead tissue or any that is damaged. Most of those bacteria are fairly unspecialized, which is why this was able to adapt to us, probably. That should be enough, Red. Let's see if we can match it with an antibody."

With the equipment they had, that was a long process, though Wilson expected to finish it before the day was over. Each specimen had to be prepared and examined individually under the microscope. It was about as unexciting to watch as it could be. Bob stuck around for a while and then went back with Kirby to the house. He had to refile all the cards and get them back to Sanchez.

"It's fine he can learn what causes and stops the plague,"

Kirby admitted, when they were back in the house. "But how does that save anybody?"

"It may not. Sometimes it's difficult to synthesize an antibody. But nowadays, it usually is possible to analyze one and get it into production pretty quickly. Then the synthetic antibody can be given to anyone at the first symptom, and the disease will be under control."

"Yeah. Reminds me of the time Davy Dreadnaught got tired of going so far between planets." Kirby moved into the kitchen, his voice rising over the sound of dinner preparations. "Davy figured it out. Trouble was the planet orbits were all spread out. If they could be stacked one on top of the other, they'd need a lot less space. Then a ship would only have to go up and down, 'stead of all around. Of course, planet orbits are slippery—they have to be for the planets to slip around them without losing speed. But that could be fixed with glue. So he got a bunch of his boys together with their ships, and they pried up the orbits as careful as they could. Orbits used to be real circles, and Davy didn't want to change their shape. They pried them up easy and gentle and lifted them into position. Mercury at the top and Pluto at the bottom. They stacked them up like pancakes, and then the other ships came in and sprayed the glue on them. It was a right pretty thing to see. Only there was one little trouble."

He waited until Bob asked the expected question and then came to the door, nodding solemnly. "The glue wasn't heatproof. It melted, being so close to the sun, and all those orbits went slipping out of position. You can see the evidence any time you look close—none of the orbits is a real circle any more, and Pluto's way out of line."

"So you think maybe the glue will come unstuck in Dad's efforts?" Bob asked. But Kirby was busy making so much noise with a beater that he might not have heard. Bob wondered whether the old man was right. It would be just their luck to have this one of the antibodies that would take months for a team of scientists to analyze.

But when his father came in, he held out a slide, carefully labeled. Now, at least, they knew which particular antibody was necessary.

It was a somewhat more cheerful dinner than most had been. They were debating whether to announce the progress when there was a bang against the entrance. Kirby answered, and even his face was split into a wide smile.

"Supply capsule is due in," he announced. "Larry caught its approach signal and he's in the control shack to key it down. Maybe this is going to be a good day all around."

They all went out to watch the capsule come in. It had been sent out from Earth by an unmanned rocket at far more acceleration than any human pilot could take. It had coasted most of the way on momentum, and now it would be ready to start blasting back to landing speed. But nothing sent so far could be aimed perfectly, and the receiving end had to be ready to take control from the ground and guide it in by a radio beam.

Everyone who could walk was out at the edge of the colony now, staring across toward the crude landing field. They could make out the figure of Larry Coccagna in the little radio tower, ready to guide the capsule down, as he'd brought others down in the past. But nearly all eyes were on the black sky above the field, waiting for the first sign of the rocket blast.

It seemed to take forever. Bob glanced at his watch and saw that less than five minutes had passed since he had left the house, but it felt more like an hour. This would probably be the last shipment from Earth, but it contained huge amounts of the needed vitamin and enough uranium to operate their pile for a year. With that, they'd find some way to continue their existence.

Then, far out, there was the sudden spurt of the great rocket exhaust. Some of the speed had been lost in the long trip against the Sun's gravity, but most of it still had to be killed. It took a powerful rocket to drive such vessels.

But the blast was behaving perfectly, driving out toward them and beginning to slant slightly as steering rockets responded to messages from the ground.

Then something seemed to go wrong. There was a prolonged blast from a steering rocket that sent the capsule's main blast into an unnatural angle, far out of the landing path. There was another blast, apparently to correct for the first, but it went even wilder.

Sanchez was running across the field toward the radio tower, waving his arms wildly. A number of others began pelting after him, and Bob found himself with the rest.

The rocket was going crazy. Some effort was still being made to control it, obviously, by fits and starts, but the results were only worse than what had been going on before. The ship was still losing speed, but it was veering off toward the side. Then the side blasts stopped as the fuel ran out. A moment later, the main blast came to an end. Now the rocket could not be seen, but its course had already been spotted well enough.

It would miss Ganymede by a wide distance and head off toward the side of Jupiter. Bob knew that it was going slowly enough now not to pass the giant planet, but it would probably take a highly elliptic orbit.

It might as well have been set to crash into Jupiter for all the good it would do the colonists. Even with the space tug, there was no chance now of overtaking it. In a few more minutes, it would probably be impossible to locate it, since no exact record of its path had been possible.

They raced across the field toward the tower and Larry Coccagna. Now Dr. McCarthy was in the front, along with Sanchez. They sprang up the ladder toward the little room in the tower, while the rest waited below.

By the time Bob reached the base, the two were already bringing the mayor's nephew down. He was dangling limply in their arms, and the brilliant fever-red of his face told all that was needed. For once, Larry had been sticking to his job, and it had still turned out wrong. The attack must have hit him while he was waiting for the ship. He hadn't been able to take time even to signal for help. He'd had to stick to his post, trying to force himself not to pass out or lose control of himself. And he'd almost made it. If he could have held out five more minutes, the ship would have landed safely.

The crowd made an ugly, united sound and started forward, as if to tear Larry to bits. Then the mood seemed to change as they got a closer look at his face. They drew back slowly, to let Sanchez and McCarthy carry him back toward the hospital. There was fear on the onlooking faces now, instead of fury. Fear and dull hopelessness. Other men could operate the normal radio equipment, but only Coccagna had been trained to handle a rocket by remote radio control.

Somewhere toward Jupiter, the capsule with the desperately needed supplies drifted farther and farther away.

12 / Desperation

THE COLONY SEEMED ALMOST deserted the next day. Most of the work had stopped. It seemed useless to go on with it, and it would have placed more drain on their power supply. Without the uranium slugs from the capsule, it seemed that there would soon be no power even for light, heat, and air replacement. Sanchez had admitted that the slugs in their power pile were already badly contaminated and that power would be falling from now on. Maybe they could still get by for six weeks, or two months at the most. After that, there would be no hope for anyone.

Earth had been contacted. The government had finally agreed to send out another unmanned capsule, this one to be charged against the colony. But without Coccagna, who was to bring it down? The man was desperately sick.

"He'll recover," McCarthy told a hastily convened group of the older colonists.

There were surprised looks from the small council, but they took his word for it. It offered very little hope at best, however. When the meeting broke up, the men left for their own homes, acting like whipped dogs.

Dan Kirby watched them leave, his old eyes studying the slumped shoulders and beaten faces of the men he had known for years. He sighed. "I been to a lot of places, but I never saw anything like that from frontier people. Well, maybe like the old superstition, you can't kill a snake till sundown—but that doesn't apply when you keep beating him to a pulp. I reckon they've been hit once too often. Doc, did you mean that about Larry Coccagna?"

"I meant it," McCarthy said. He grimaced. "I think the man's the worst troublemaker we have here, but he also happens to be necessary if there's to be any hope for us all. So I gave him the last of the antibody from Bob's blood."

He went out toward the hospital, looking almost as beaten as the other men. Dr. Wilson was already at the laboratory. Now he seemed to be the only hope left. He had reached the stage where Red was no help to him, since the theory of what he was seeking was too far advanced for anyone else in the colony.

The long day dragged on. Bob spent some time at the laboratory, ready to help if he could. At this stage, he was more familiar with his father's methods than Red was. But there was nothing he could do beyond bringing lunch for his father.

On a large chart there was a diagram of the antibody. Most of it was filled in now, and Wilson pointed to it. "So far, it's routine. But there are two large gaps. I don't know what I'll find there. If it's what I hope, we can begin synthesizing the stuff in a couple of days. Red knows enough engineering to make the setup for me. But if it's what I'm beginning to believe it is, I don't think we have a chance."

Bob looked over the maze of equipment. Some of it was crude, and some consisted of the gifts from the scientists on the ship. But it meant almost nothing to him. Biochemistry had spent almost two centuries in developing methods for finding out the complicated structure of the giant living molecules, and that technique couldn't be learned merely from helping out as a child. It was a severe discipline, so difficult that only men with exceptional minds and special gifts could master it.

By evening, Dr. Wilson was finished. Bob found him putting his equipment away, and moved to help him. His father's face was set in lines of strain. Bob had begun to watch him for signs of the plague, since he'd never been exposed to the milder form and should have been more susceptible. But there was no evidence of it yet.

Wilson refused to talk about it until they were all back at the house. Then he spread his hands in defeat.

"It's hopeless for us," he reported. "I have it analyzed, but we can't synthesize it. There is one step in the building up of the molecule that is almost impossible. It can occur only under extreme pressures—on the order of twenty thousand pounds a square inch. On Earth, there are places where that can be handled, but we couldn't remotely approximate it here."

"It's made in the human body without such pressures," McCarthy objected. Then he twisted his lips at his own reasoning. "Sorry. That doesn't mean anything. There are a lot of things that our bodies do in ways we can't duplicate outside the cell walls. I should have known better."

Bob got up and left them. There was nothing he could

add to the conversation, and he felt the need for a walk—for anything to take his mind off the pressure of fear around him. Apparently Red had the same idea, since he was dressing as Bob passed his door.

Penny came running out, her face serious and worried. "Take me with you," she pleaded. "I've got to go. I've got to see them again. They're waiting for me."

Red frowned at her. "You stay here, squirt, and don't add to your father's worries. Things are bad enough without your running off."

They left her in her room and went out onto the street. Now a few people were moving about, heading toward the shed where they had held their meeting. Bob moved toward them, expecting to receive black looks, but there were only apathetic nods of greeting. It was apparently no formal meeting but simply a bunch of worried people, hoping that somehow by coming together, someone could give them something they could no longer supply for themselves.

Then, suddenly, there were gasps. Red looked upward and jerked at Bob's arm. He swung about, just as the object came fully over the horizon.

It was the globe ship, flying very low and slowly. It came toward the colony from the south, seemed to hesitate, and then moved directly over the houses of the people. For a minute it stood still, as if looking at the crowd below.

There were yells in a confused jumble in Bob's radio, and a few started to run. But most simply stood and looked upward, unable to believe what they saw. One woman was on her knees, her arms raised in pleading. She probably thought it was a rescue ship from Earth.

The globe lifted finally and moved off toward the north. It seemed to be flying uncertainly, Bob noticed.

Sanchez was among them too late. He had caught only a glimpse of the ship, but he was giving orders for posting guards. And word was spreading that it was an enemy ship of some sort. Here and there, a man claimed to have seen it before, always when Jupiter was directly over them. The story of danger was growing as word was passed from one man to another. Now even those who had not seen it, but had come in answer to frantic urging from others, were adding their speculations.

One man had an old rifle, and he brought it out proudly. It was obviously the only weapon in the colony. Sanchez promptly posted him to do guard duty.

Bob and Red turned back to their house, but there was no need to report. The others of the household were standing outside, still staring at the place where the globe had disappeared. They must have come out in time to see some of its performance.

Back inside, Red began reporting what he'd discovered the night they followed Penny. It would have been exciting news once, but now it came as an anticlimax. Everyone had seen the globe, and there was no doubt of its reality.

"What difference does it make?" McCarthy summed up their reactions. "If it has been appearing regularly for four years without doing any harm here, there's no reason to be excited about it now. We'll probably have to send out a group of men to explore the place where Penny meets it, but that can wait until the men cool down. Right now, I wouldn't trust them."

Dr. Wilson nodded agreement. "I realize, of course, that this is like the one Bob saw attacking the *Procyon*. But if your daughter can talk to them at all, I'm willing to accept her account of that attack. Where is she now?"

"She's in her room, crying because I won't let her go out," Mrs. McCarthy answered. "I just left there a few minutes ago. Maybe I'd better bake her a cake. She likes cake, and she hasn't had any for a week."

"Better keep an eye on her," the doctor suggested. "I've got to get back to the hospital. Noel, are you going to try to reach Earth tonight?"

The scientist nodded. "If I can find one of the men who can operate the radio."

"Reckon I can do that," Kirby volunteered. "We had to learn about that when I was on the *Taft*, and these rigs haven't changed much since then. But you'll get poor reception, Dr. Wilson. We're on the wrong side of Jupiter, and we'll have to relay through Callisto."

"We'll try it anyhow," Wilson decided.

He went into the laboratory to get his notes in order for transmission to Earth. Kirby stood staring back toward the north.

"Callisto relay reminds me of something," he told Bob. "I was there on the first expedition. Nasty little moon, so light a man can't really set his feet down. We always wondered why it was so light till we got there. Then we found it was all full of holes and tunnels—practically hollow. You reckon those people in the globe mined out all its ore once?"

"It would mean they've been in space a long time,

137

wouldn't it? Callisto's mass was discovered back in the twentieth century."

"So? Maybe they were around long before that. Maybe a few of those old flying saucer stories were true. Oh, mostly I guess they were nonsense, but I heard a few when I was a kid that almost made me believe 'em."

Bob found it hard to believe that there could be any relation between this ship and the fantasies of the past. It seemed more likely that the globes had stayed near Jupiter and that they had known nothing about men until Earth began colonizing.

Dr. Wilson came out finally, and they headed toward the radio shack. The man with the rifle was patrolling along the edge of Outpost, trying to look less scared than he obviously was. Sooner or later, he would probably shoot at somebody and add to their other troubles.

But he gave them no trouble as they moved across the landing field. The radio tower was a small structure, with its antenna raised as high as possible above the level of the ground. There was barely room inside for all three, and the air supply was not designed for that many people. Bob moved his valve on his oxygen bottle a trifle, enriching the air they were breathing.

Kirby studied the simple little instrument board of the transmitter and nodded. He threw a switch, and the board lighted. From somewhere in one of the drawers, he found a manual key and plugged it in. "Better use code—it's easier to read when reception is bad," he decided. He wiggled his fingers, tapping the key a couple of times, and began adjusting

138

the small dish-shaped antenna. Finally he nodded. "I'm in contact with the automatic relay on Callisto."

Bob had never seen code sent before, and for a few minutes the tapping of dots and dashes fascinated him. He had heard it, and he knew that Kirby was a little slow, but the sounds seemed as exact and precise as the old man's handwriting.

It was a long message, full of repeats in case some was lost in the transmission. And there was a longer wait when the old man finally finished. It took thirty-five minutes for the message to reach Earth, and another thirty-five minutes for the return message.

"Do you think they will really try to make the antibody on Earth?" Bob asked.

Wilson had no doubts, judging by his expression. "They'll make it," he stated. "They seem to be as frightened of the plague there as we are—maybe more so. There hasn't been any threat of an interplanetary plague since the Martian fever, but that seems to have made a lasting impression. The question is whether they can make it and get it to us in time to help."

An hour passed, then another went by, without any reply except a brief acknowledgment that the message had been received. Bob felt cramped, and the smoke from the men's pipes began to bother him. He curled up on a low seat, almost falling asleep.

Kirby's hand roused him. "Entertainment committee's back!"

The globe was rising over the horizon again. This time it

came up from north of the village, probably from the Bowl where they had first seen it. It rose more steeply, beginning to rush upward and out into space. But it wasn't heading toward Jupiter this time. It was taking a path that would bring it far off to the side.

"Which way is Callisto?" Bob asked.

"You figure it's going to put a monkey wrench in our relay station?" Kirby asked. He calculated and shook his head. "No, can't be. Callisto's the other way."

Half an hour later, Bob saw it coming back. It seemed to wobble as it drew near Ganymede, and then it slipped behind the horizon.

"Busy night," Kirby decided. "I think I'm just going to pay a little visit out there when I get time."

His musings were interrupted by the click of the sounder on the board. He flipped a couple of switches and made microscopic adjustments on a dial, until a fair signal seemed to be coming through the speaker.

Kirby read it off as it came over, translating the Morse into slow words. "They've studied your description and believe antibody can be made. Something, something—oh. It's all being repeated three times. Yeah. They are going to try immediately, but it's a slow and expensive process. They cannot hope to deliver antibody for colony for—umm, wait —for three weeks plus time of capsule in space. Some name I can't get congratulates you for brilliant work, Dr. Wilson."

The signal ended, and Wilson groaned. Three weeks to get the antibody and at least six more to ship it to Ganymede. The colony could never wait that long for help.

140

"I reckon we're still on our own," Kirby decided.

"It seems we are," Wilson agreed bitterly.

They climbed down the tower ladder and headed back for the house. By mutual consent, they did not intend to report this to Sanchez. There was no point in adding one more piece of bitter irony to the fate that hung over the colony.

McCarthy was still at the hospital, supervising the care of two new patients who had just come in. By now, most of the beds were filled. There were nearly thirty people suffering from the plague. So far, three besides Bob had recovered, and eleven had died. The doctor listened to Wilson's report on the call to Earth with tight lips but no surprise. He turned back to his work as soon as he'd heard the news, and the others went out again.

There was the sound of crying as soon as they entered the house. Bob saw Mrs. McCarthy standing in the living room, dabbing at her eyes with her apron. Beyond her, Red was buckling on his suit.

"It's Penny," Red said. "She's sneaked out again. Aunt Maude just woke me up to tell me."

"But she promised," Mrs. McCarthy insisted. "She promised if I'd bake her the cake, she would go right to sleep and not stir from her room."

"She'll be all right." Bob tried to assure the woman. "She isn't lost, and we'll find her."

He wasn't as confident as he tried to sound, however. With all the strange activity of the globe ship, he couldn't be sure what would happen to Penny out there.

13 / The Supply Capsule

"HOW LONG HAS SHE been gone?" Dr. Wilson asked.

Mrs. McCarthy shook her head, and her voice was muffled as she brought the apron up to her eyes again. "I don't know. I just don't know, Dan. She never disobeyed me before and now——"

Kirby snorted. "Seems to me she's been disobeying you regular for four years, ma'am," he said firmly. "And if she hasn't been killed doing it so far, I guess she'll live this time. Even if she comes down with plague out there—" He stopped as she gasped in shock at the idea, then went on. "If she comes down with it out there, she's no worse off than she would be here. Bob and I can bring her back. Red, I think maybe you better stay here with your aunt."

Surprisingly, Mrs. McCarthy seemed to calm down at hearing the worst. Red protested at staying behind, but he seemed secretly relieved as he began climbing out of his vacuum suit. He looked tired.

Bob and Kirby stopped at the storeroom to attach fresh oxygen tanks to their suits. The old man shook his head unhappily. "Penny is a nice little tyke, but she's been spoiled

142

rotten. She was born after Maude McCarthy gave up hope of having a child, so I reckon her mother thinks she's some sort of a miracle." He strapped a third bottle of oxygen onto his shoulders. "Might as well have a spare for her. Reckon you can find the way, Bob?"

"I guess I can," Bob decided. He had been worrying about something else. He didn't want to think about it, but the possibility had to be faced. "Why didn't you want Red along? Do you think he's coming down with the plague?"

"Dunno. But I don't like what I see, and I'll bet your father is worried, too; that's the real reason he didn't want Red helping him today. Could be he's one of the slow cases."

They went out again and headed north. Bob was trying to remember how long Red had been looking so tired, and worry was deepening in him. Sometimes the plague struck quickly, as in the case of Coccagna; but other cases matured very slowly, and Red could be one of those.

They reached the edge of Outpost. The man with the rifle came running up, crying out a challenge to them. "You can't go that way. Nobody goes there till we decide what to do."

"You going to stop me, Jake?" Kirby asked. "You sure you want to try that popgun against someone who really knows how to use it?"

"It's for your own good, Dan," the man protested. "I got orders not to let anyone go where they might get hurt. You gotta stay here until Mr. Sanchez decides what to do about that globe."

"You gonna stop me?" Kirby asked again.

Jake worried, moving the rifle unhappily in his hands.

Finally he shrugged. "Okay, Dan, get yourself killed then. It's your business."

"That's right, Jake. It *is* my business," Kirby said firmly. He sighed unhappily as they moved along the rocky ground. "Looks like I'll have to run for mayor again, if we ever live through this. Sanchez started fine, but he's getting the old politician's disease—he's afraid to trust the people. Government is designed to protect people when they can't handle things themselves, Bob. It's never meant to protect them *from* themselves. That's their own business. And when any man in authority forgets that, it's time to replace him."

They moved along steadily. Bob found that his memory of the trail was clearer than he'd expected, and there seemed little chance of making any serious error. He set a steady pace, not trying to hurry too much, since a few minutes' difference would hardly matter. At what he judged to be the halfway point, he motioned toward a large, flat rock and dropped down on it. The old man sank down beside him.

"Don't you ever get tired?" Bob asked him.

Kirby sighed, and then a slow grin crept over his face. "Bob, I'm just about dead on my feet right now. Sure I get tired. And I get scared, too. Only I've kind of learned to live with it. Took me fifty years to find that a man can keep going after he feels tired, or can manage to act normal when he's afraid, but he can. Trouble with most people is that they spoil themselves—the minute something is a little hard, they give up. Then next time, it gets hard sooner. They get in the habit of babying themselves. I've seen men who kept quitting a little sooner each time, and pretty soon they were plumb tuckered out just from breathing. Bob?"

"Yeah, Dan?" He used the first name without thinking, and then realized it and was embarrassed. He'd been taught respect for his elders.

But Kirby chuckled and dropped a metal-clad hand on his arm. "I like that, boy. I like it real fine. But what I was going to say is that you have to get used to us old people passing on what we've learned about life to you youngsters. I used to try not to do it, but now I kind of feel I should. It's the best we can do for you. And if any of what we say ever helps you, we're going to be mighty tickled. But just remember it's only the way we see things, and we may be wrong. It's up to you to use what you can—and, I guess, to listen politely to the rest of it. Come on, let's get going."

They began the upward climb through the gorge and to the lip of the Bowl. Bob avoided the short cut Red had taken and followed the easier path this time. As they neared the top, there was a flicker of movement, and he saw Penny coming around a bend.

She hadn't seen them, but her helmet radio was on, and he heard her sniffling. Her head was lowered, and she was trudging along as if the whole world had failed her. Then she looked up and saw him. This time, she seemed almost glad. She came forward more quickly.

"They won't talk any more," she said miserably. "And I can't make them do anything right. There's something *awful* wrong, Bob. I know there is. They don't like me any more."

"Nobody else is going to like you much either, young one, if you keep up this running off," Kirby told her. "You're old enough to stop acting like a baby."

"I don't act like a baby!" she flared back at him.

"Nope. Reckon not. A baby usually tries to be as good as it knows how. Oh, well, I reckon you're not my problem." He turned to Bob. "I'm going to go look at that globe, if it's still there. And you can come along or take her back, whichever you feel like."

"I want to go home," Penny began.

Bob hesitated, and then cut off any further pleading from her. "We're going on to the globe. I want to see it again, too, and you can wait until we're ready to go back." A few minutes more wouldn't add much worry to her family, and they really should report on the ship, if they could learn anything.

Penny hung back until she saw they meant it and then followed along meekly enough. Bob agreed with Kirby's opinion of her; she was much too used to having her own way, but she was basically a very nice kid.

"I'd better go first and tell them, so they won't be scared when they see you," she warned the two men.

The idea of two unarmed humans scaring the globe seemed ridiculous, but Bob remembered that the ship had taken off on sighting him before. He nodded to Penny, and the girl began trotting down the slope.

The globe was resting almost where it had been before. The three smaller spheres were down on the ground, and there was something between them, almost hidden in the inky shadows. But there was no sign of the glowing panel, and the little opening was closed. No change appeared as Penny ran up to the ship and began scrawling hasty lines on it. There was no response.

This time the ship made no move to take off as the two

men appeared. Bob had a better chance to study it. There seemed to be no break in the smooth surface. He had no idea how thick the metal walls were, or of what they were made, but there was a suggestion of massive strength about it.

Kirby grunted suddenly. His breath sucked in sharply. "Bob. Take a good look at what's under the thing!"

Bob moved around to where the old man stood. Here there was some reflection of light from nearby rocks, and he could make out an outline of the object between the supports. He stared at it unbelievingly, moving closer until there could be no doubt.

The object was the supply capsule that had been sent out from Earth!

It was held above the ground, locked to the bottom of the great globe between the supporting spheres. Some kind of a metal grapple held it firmly in place.

Penny had come around beside them. "That's what I sent them to get," she said.

For once, Kirby seemed completely taken aback. He straightened and stared at the girl in astonishment. "You sent them out to get the capsule? Just like that?"

"No. Not exactly." She frowned unhappily. "It was kind of hard, and they acted funny. But then they went out where it was—they knew where, I didn't. And they brought it back here."

That would account for the trip out and back that Bob had seen from the radio tower. He moved back from the ship to a place where he could sit down, pulling her with him. "I think you'd better tell us the whole story, Penny," he suggested.

It came out in a rather garbled form. She had a habit of taking too much for granted or of jumping about. But eventually he drew it out of her, with help from Kirby.

She hadn't been able to get away the night they usually came, though she'd tried. And tonight, she'd been caught again. The ship must have grown tired of waiting for her. At least, it had done something it hadn't tried before. It had swung over Outpost and signaled her. Apparently the plastic sheet Red had found in her room lighted up whenever the ship was near. But this time, as it passed over the colony, the sheet had sent her a message. According to her, it was a funny message but awfully important looking.

When she'd finally reached the Bowl, carrying her presents for them, they hadn't bothered to open the door. They didn't want the metal this time. They wanted something else, and she couldn't understand what. Then she'd told them about the supply capsule and asked them to get it. She'd been planning on that ever since the capsule was lost, knowing they could find it.

"They got awful excited, and went so fast I couldn't keep up," she said, pointing to the panel where the stick signals had appeared. "Then they slowed down, but it was all funny. I couldn't make any sense of it. So I just kept telling them about the capsule over and over. Then they went out and got it."

"Well, it's quite a ways to the colony," Kirby said. "But I reckon people will be pretty glad to come out and drag it back somehow. You did a fine thing, Penny. Now tell them to release it."

148

She started to cry again, quietly. "I tried and tried and tried. But they won't. They just sit there, and they don't even make the pictures or anything. See!"

She went back and began drawing against the side of the ship. Nothing happened.

Bob moved beside her. "Tell them it's important to us, Penny. Tell them we are dying—"

"I can't—can't make that!"

"All right. Tell them we are going like this, then." He reached up to the place where her hands had been and made a sine wave that gradually faded out—a series of waves that got smaller and smaller and stopped.

Immediately the big panel began to glow. The figure Bob had drawn was reproduced, while something that might have been a picture of Penny appeared beside it.

Penny squealed in delight. "You're smart, Bob. Now I can tell them." She began drawing her lines as fast as she could move her hands. Other sticks seemed to move on the great panel. The damped wave train that Bob had drawn was also mixed into it.

Bob realized it was the first practical use he had ever made of all the analytic linguistics he had studied. But what could be a more universal symbol of death than that? In a way, though, it confirmed his guess that the creatures on board the globe thought in processes and relationships, rather than in separate things.

Penny turned back. She was frowning again.

"They know now. But they are—unhappy. They want something, but not metal. I don't know what they say now. And I think they can't get back home."

"If their ship is in trouble, I don't know what we can do. But we could try to help, I guess," Bob told her.

"The ship can go back. They can't," she said.

A group of exiles from their own world? Bob couldn't make sense of the pictures that flashed on the screen nor the complicated curves that ran across it. Penny made even less sense from that part. There was something wrong with each curve, Bob saw. They must be indicating some trouble, but he couldn't guess what. How could a human being imagine what would be trouble to a non-human?

Finally the panel went blank, except for the two lines that moved on it. And even those seemed curiously uncertain and shaky. Then the panel darkened completely.

"They won't make any more," Penny said. It was curious construction that would have been more natural in French, but might also be the closest translation from the signs.

She was right. Nothing he could do would produce any answer. Nor would they release the capsule. It rested firmly in the grapples, which were strong enough to resist any effort the colony could make.

"I suppose we could try blasting the capsule open with explosives, if the globe would stay put for that," Kirby said. "I can't see any other answer. One of those things has got the loading port closed tight in its grip."

Bob felt reluctant to make any move that might be considered hostile, but they might have to try blasting the capsule free, he realized—provided the globe stayed where it was long enough. They had to report to the colony, at least.

Penny was quiet as they started back. She trudged wearily along, trying to keep up, until Kirby picked her up in his arms and slung her across his shoulders, piggyback style.

"Better hurry," he decided. "We don't know how long that thing will wait, and we'd better get men back here fast."

They moved as rapidly as they could. The old man might be as tired as he had said before, but he kept up with the best speed Bob could manage. They went up the edge of the Bowl and started down the gorge.

Something passed over their heads, making a great shadow on the ground. Bob jerked his head up to see the globe, flying very low and slowly. It seemed to be uncertain, or else it was hard to keep it at that height. It veered off toward the west, rising just barely over the hills there, and then disappeared behind them.

The capsule had still been gripped underneath it.

"Looks like we failed again," Kirby said.

Bob nodded glumly. He couldn't expect the globe to sit there waiting, he supposed. Whatever bargaining the creatures had tried to do with it hadn't worked out, and they were moving it elsewhere. It would be easy to take it back to space where nobody could find it. Or the ship could simply move part way across the little moon and drop the capsule where no man could find it in time to save them. They had been given the chance, and they had failed. Or he had failed!

Then the globe appeared again, coming back over the gorge in which they were moving. It seemed to wobble more this time, as if some clumsy student were piloting it. Bob swung around to follow its progress, and groaned as it seemed certain to strike the edge of the Bowl. At the last moment, it lifted and passed over, to drop quickly from sight.

"No capsule this time," Kirby said. "They must have ditched it somewhere."

It didn't help much. Even in the short time the globe had been gone, it could have covered enough miles to put the capsule out of reach of the colony. They would have to send out search parties, Bob supposed, but it would be just one more futile hope piled on top of other ruined chances. And the ship could always move in to snatch the capsule out of their reach if it realized they were close to the right place.

There was no use in hurrying now. He moved along beside the old man, hardly seeing the trail they followed back to Outpost.

14 / Friendly Gesture

FROM HALF A MILE away, Bob could see that Outpost was in a frenzy of excitement. Everyone seemed to be outside in the streets. The biggest cluster of people was at the south end of the colony, but human figures could be seen everywhere, milling about, with some on the run.

His first thought was that the globe had attacked the colony. But there was no sign of damage that he could see. He turned up the gain on his helmet radio, and sounds began to come in, but they were such a babble of different voices that he could make no sense of it.

He had broken into a clumsy run, and Kirby was trotting along beside him.

He shouted now, trying to get their attention, but no one seemed to hear.

A suspicion of the truth was beginning to enter his mind now, however. He managed to increase his speed a trifle. It seemed incredible, but everything else about the globe was equally fantastic. Yet there was no other good explanation.

Kirby shouted for him to go on, that he'd take Penny back to her parents. But there was no need for them to separate. Bob spotted Dr. McCarthy in the group at the end of the street, and pointed. Mrs. McCarthy was also there, he saw.

And now he could see that his hopes were confirmed. Lying in the middle of a confused crowd of people was the supply capsule! The creatures in the globe hadn't been trying to keep it out of reach. They had made the ultimate friendly gesture. Unable to make whatever bargain they had hoped for, they had risked everything they feared from the humans of the colony to bring the capsule to those who needed it, and to release it within easy reach!

And they'd also shown an understanding that was greater than Bob's had been. They had understood his message to them fully, though he had been unable to decode theirs.

Kirby handed Penny to her mother and joined Bob as he reached the main group. The capsule was already open, and Dr. McCarthy was drawing out the big packages of medical supplies. They had been sealed for space handling and could not be hurt by exposure to the vacuum here. The doctor broke open one pack and began handing out small plastic bottles. He thrust one to Bob, who saw that it was labeled as one hundred tablets of vitamin C.

Sanchez came running up importantly, but Kirby beat him to the punch. "You can thank Penny for this, Luis," the old man announced. "She's the one who got them to bring this thing back. She can talk to them."

Men near by picked up the words and began passing the facts around. There was another wave of excitement now. Penny was suddenly the center of attention, while Sanchez was forgotten. The mayor looked crestfallen for a moment, then grinned.

"You always could beat me, Dan," he conceded. "I should have known you'd be mixed up in this. Come on where we can talk and maybe we can put both sides together."

There wasn't a great deal they could learn from the mayor. The ship had come in low from the west. Most people were inside and didn't see it, but Sanchez had been out talking to Jake, the guard. The globe had hovered uncertainly and then had touched down on the only clear space big enough to hold it. Jake had gone running off, firing his rifle.

"You'd better take that away from him," Kirby suggested.

"I already got it. Anyhow, he only had one load for it. But the old fool should have looked first to see where he was firing. He could have killed people."

No harm had been done. Sanchez had seen the bullets bounce off the ship and ricochet around, but the globe had probably not even been aware of them. It was already rising. It swooped up maybe two hundred feet, began to twist over, and then scooted back for the north. When they reached the place where it had been, they found the capsule. The performance was all over before most people knew the globe had been there.

Sanchez listened more attentively as Kirby described what they had seen and done. "I guess we get more help from Jupiter than Earth," he said at last. "Okay, maybe I send some men out with the girl tomorrow and we try to figure out again what they want. If we got it, they can have it."

The colony overreacted to the first good thing that had happened to them. McCarthy watched them with worry in his eyes, but he made no effort to stop their celebration. They needed it.

In his own house, though, he let his pessimism show again. "I hope the vitamin dosage I've given helps," he told Dr. Wilson. "But I'm doubtful of it. Oh, maybe it will increase our resistance to the disease to some extent, or even save a few people who might die otherwise. But it's too late to hope that it will prevent the plague. When we had the milder form of the disease, a good shot of ascorbic acid was enough to let a man throw it off. But this stuff is pretty well settled by now. I suspect every one of us who hasn't already had the virulent form is incubating it."

"I thought it had a short incubation period," Bob said. He had supposed that his own exposure and attack were separated by only a couple of days.

"Sometimes it acts that way," McCarthy admitted. "But I've had plague cells in my own blood for quite a while. I checked on that as soon as we knew which ones were dangerous. And nothing has happened yet. We don't know enough yet to be sure what does trigger it into full action."

Bob watched Red carefully, but he could see no sign of the plague now. The boy had taken a massive dose of the vitamin, but he had already looked better after the sleep he had managed to get while they were gone.

The next morning found seven fresh patients. The hospital was filled now, and the women who served as nurses were busy. It was more than McCarthy could handle, and he drafted Wilson to assist him. The scientist was no medical

156

doctor, but he had had to learn a fair amount about disease, and he was no longer needed for his own research. That had reached a dead end.

The colony was somewhat sobered as people began to realize that only the normal emergencies of short supplies and danger to their power were over. The menace of the plague remained. But the relief of having even one friendly gesture from a universe that had seemed completely hostile, left them more able to face that danger.

There were plenty of volunteers for the trip up to the Bowl that day. Sanchez picked out Kirby and Bob to go with Penny, and appointed himself as the driver of the little tractor that would carry them this time. He was pulling a small trailer that was loaded with everything that anyone could think to send. There were tools, metal of all the kinds they had in the colony, chemicals from the processing plants, and even samples of the drugs that had come in the supply capsule. As a final effort of good will, Sanchez had brought one of the uranium slugs in the radiation-proof container in which it was shipped.

Bob had expected Penny to be in her glory as queen of the day. But she surprised him. She was interested only in getting up to "them" and trying to re-establish communications. Bob remembered his thoughts of her being a pet of theirs. In a way, it fitted; she was acting like a puppy too long separated from its master. Or maybe it was the other way around, and she thought the globe creatures were her pets!

He realized now that there was another lack in all the languages he knew. There was no word to describe any relationship between different forms of life that gave dignity to both. A pet was not the equal of its keeper. A symbiote was something that existed in a physical relation with another, but not with any understanding. And men had always meant humans when they referred to friends. He couldn't honestly call the creatures in the globe friends, since that would require more knowledge and understanding than they had.

The globe was still there as the tractor maneuvered its way down the rocky, tricky trail. Sanchez was a good driver, though, and he brought them safely to a stop beside the globe.

There was no response from it. It simply sat there. Penny went to the panel and labored over her messages, but the larger panel remained blank.

She seemed sure that the creatures inside could see out in some manner, and Bob agreed with her. They could hardly have made even the distorted pictures of things without some ability to see the objects. Sanchez and Kirby unpacked the trailer, holding one object after another up for inspection. The door remained closed in the hull.

Then abruptly the panel glowed. Two lines appeared and jerked uncertainly. Penny frowned as she studied them. The lines moved slowly, almost fumblingly. Once there was a track of blackness over the whole panel, as if something were being canceled, then the lines started to move again, repeating almost the same patterns.

"They say no," Penny translated.

"Just that—no?" Sanchez asked.

She nodded. Then the lines began again.

"They—they want the one who—who . . . I think they mean you, Bob," she said at last.

He moved up to the panel, touching it. Above him, there was a vague wiggle of curves. He had a sense of the ridiculousness of what his only explanation was, but he could think of nothing better. Penny had been a baby, almost, when they first contacted her. And they had invented a kind of baby talk, using the simplest symbols. But now he had used a curve, which was apparently closer to their language, and they were hoping he could be treated as an adult. He knew bitterly that he must disappoint them.

There was something labored and clumsy about the picture that took shape, but Bob finally realized it was supposed to be the globe itself. Then it grew hazy, and a number of things appeared inside. There was no true shape to them —only a series of writhing lines and vague colors. The globe slowly faded from around them, and over them appeared the symbol of the damped wave train Bob had used before.

The picture remained as the doorway opened in the side of the globe. It opened only part way, remaining open just a second. The curved symbol filled out and then went back to its former shape as the door closed.

Bob had underestimated them. Somehow, they'd managed to tell him at least part of what they wanted him to know. He sighed and went back to the others.

"They're in trouble, all right. And the trouble isn't with the ship. They are dying in there, or I think they are. And they want help. They think we can give them something that can save them, or they're asking us to try. That's what they meant by opening the door. But I guess they have no way of saying what they need."

"You mean they're sick—like us?" Sanchez asked.

Bob nodded. It was the best interpretation he could make. And Penny also nodded, tears in her eyes.

"Yes." She nodded slowly to herself, her eyes on the globe. "They told me they were all—wrong. It was. . . . Going back to their place was bad. Do you think they'll all die, Bob?"

"I don't know, Penny," he told her.

It all fitted together, though there was always a chance that at least half of his guesses were wrong. But the ship had been flown badly, as it might if some very sick pilot were handling it. And the symbol he had used for death was one he felt sure they understood. Now they had used it for themselves. Maybe they were dying here because they were unable to get home again. Maybe there was some plague on Jupiter and these were the only survivors, looking desperately for help. Or maybe the truth was something he could never fully understand. But the creatures inside the ship were sick and desperate.

He felt sick inside himself and in every cell of his body. Man and alien had finally met, after all these years in space. They had even established some kind of communication, and they wanted to be friendly. But the men were a small group dying of the plague and the aliens were also dying inside their ship. There was no help for either, it seemed.

He moved to the panel again. His finger went out and touched it, making a dot. He couldn't know whether they would understand, but it was the least developed figure possible, and they might know it expressed the limits of human ability to help—no development, no extension, no dimension.

There was a long wait. Then the two lines appeared, blended together, and grew shorter and shorter until they were only a dot.

They'd understood. And they were saying good-by as best they could.

He told Sanchez what it had meant. The man stood looking at the ship. "I'm crying," he said.

And there were tears in his eyes.

Bob wished vaguely that the creatures in the globe could have known that someone like Sanchez could cry for them. But maybe in their own way, they could cry for humans, too.

The panel remained blank. Sanchez looked at the goods on the trailer and shrugged. He uncoupled the trailer and left it behind. The stuff was useless to the Jovians, but maybe they could accept the gesture.

"We don't tell the people about this," he decided. "They got trouble enough. We say we left things beside the ship and let it go at that, eh?"

Kirby nodded. "For once, I think you're right, Luis. And I'm not sure whether I'm sorry or glad I know what really happened."

Sanchez let them out at the entrance to the house and drove off in the tractor. Bob inspected Penny, but she was trying to smile, and the tears hadn't streaked her face.

"I'll be good," she promised.

He nodded and went in with her. There was no one in the parlor, however, and he felt some relief at that. She could go to her room to get out of the suit and wash her face. There seemed to be no one else in the house. By the time the family came back, Penny would probably have gotten over most of her grief. Things didn't hurt less at her age, but recovery was quicker.

He went into his own room, slipping out of his suit. He felt drained, as if something inside had gone out of him. At the moment, he couldn't even find room to worry about the plague.

He heard steps above, and then on the stairs. It was Red coming back from the laboratory or wherever he had been, but Bob had no desire to talk. He stepped back into his own room, hoping that Red would go on.

Then the boy's voice came thickly through the crack in the door. "Bob! Bob, I think you'd better get Uncle Frank. I think I've got it."

One look at the flushed face was enough to convince Bob that Red was right. The plague had waited for days to develop, but now the first fever had hit, and there was no more doubt.

Red staggered as Bob sprang to help him, but he managed to catch his balance. "I'll be all right," he said. "I'm not as bad as you were at first. Get Uncle Frank, when he can come."

Bob bent to help remove Red's shoes. "You belong in the hospital," he objected.

"I went there," Red told him. "They were full up. Anyhow, what good can a nurse do me? I'll take my chances here and let Penny play nurse. She'll love it."

Red wasn't as bad as some had been, Bob saw. The fever was high, but there was no trace of delirium yet. This, however, was only the first phase.

15 / Fever Plan

BOB FOUND MC CARTHY IN his office after the doctor had done what he could for Red. He made his suggestion without any preamble.

"I want you to take enough blood for another dose of antibodies," he said.

McCarthy looked doubtfully at him. "You've already given all I think you should, Bob. Remember, you were sick yourself not so long ago, and I don't know whether there are aftereffects of this plague or not. Sure you know what you're doing?"

"I'm sure," Bob answered.

The doctor sighed and reached for his equipment. "Then I'm grateful, Bob. I couldn't ask for it for one of my own family, but if you volunteer, I feel a lot better. Sit over here."

The antibodies from the blood of patients who had recovered was the only reliable treatment they had. Bob felt some reaction this time, but it passed within a few minutes.

It was the wrong type for Red, which meant that it couldn't be used for a direct transfusion. It had to be put through the little centrifuge to leave only the plasma, which could be injected into any patient's blood stream. But that was a routine procedure that didn't concern Bob.

He went down to see how Red was doing. The boy was still fully conscious. Either he was having a light attack—and there had been no attack so far that didn't produce delirium —or this was building up very slowly. Penny was fussing over him. Bob was surprised to see that he seemed to enjoy it. When Bob was sick, nothing irritated him more than to have anyone doing things for him, but Red was a different sort of patient.

He went back again two hours later, trying not to be too much of a nuisance. This time he heard Penny's tongue going a mile a minute, but it stopped as he drew near. Red was lying down, but his eyes were open. He grinned weakly.

"Uncle Frank told me what you did, Bob," he said. "I think it was great. But I don't feel right in taking the antibody. There are a lot of people here who need it more than I do."

"I didn't contribute it to them," Bob said sharply. "That's between us. It's yours."

Red settled back farther into the covers, though he was sweating profusely. "Okay. In that case, I guess I'll have to admit it's mine."

He said nothing more, and Bob stood awkwardly for a few moments. Penny went to readjust the pillow—probably for the hundredth time. Bob sighed and went out again.

One of the girls who served as a nurse brought the small bottle of plasma over later. Dr. McCarthy was out on another of the calls he had to make; too many of his patients now

164

had to be left in their own homes, and it was making his harried life even more difficult. Bob took the bottle down to Red's room and put it on the table.

Red stared at it. "Life," he commented. "Funny to think a little bottle like that sitting over there six feet away can contain my life. It gives a man a feeling of disconnection."

He was still refusing to give in and sleep, and holding back the wild words of delirium was obviously harder for him now. Red's forehead was burning hot to Bob's touch. But he was stubbornly clinging to his rationality, and even going too far overboard in being impersonal about his troubles.

Bob went back upstairs, finding himself some food that he had no appetite for. He felt as if he were on a treadmill. Downstairs and upstairs, without knowing what to do in either place. He wished McCarthy could hurry back, though he knew the doctor would never delay any longer than he had to.

Then next time he started down, Penny stopped him. "He's asleep," she reported. There was a curious look to her face, but she didn't seem unusually worried. "Better not disturb him, Bob."

Bob went back to his slow pacing in the living room. He'd always hated sickness, probably because he'd had so little personal experience with it. But this was worse than any of the other times he'd had to worry about some friend.

There was the sound of the entrance lock opening, and he dashed toward it quickly, but there was no one there. He'd been sure he heard it, however; with his ears tuned to listen for the return of McCarthy, he couldn't have been mistaken.

Then he shrugged. The doctor's entrance was always

public property, and it might have been anyone. He went back down the stairs, tiptoeing to avoid waking Red. Everything was silent now.

It was too silent. He worried for a moment and then moved the door open cautiously, just a crack at first. Then he threw it fully open.

There was no one in the bed, nor was there any sign of Penny in any of the rooms!

Bob dashed for his suit and began throwing it on. He fumbled in his haste, got a grip on himself, and forced himself to move more carefully. The suit had never seemed so clumsy since the first day. Then he was dashing up the stairs toward the entrance. He had no plan, but there was a driving urgency to do something. Even the suit seemed to share his haste now.

There was no sign of Penny and Red on the street, however. He turned from side to side, hunting for any evidence, but they seemed to have disappeared. He glanced up toward the north, half expecting to see Penny moving that way, but there was no one there.

The only thing possible was to get help and start a search. Red must have gone completely delirious, and Penny must be crazy. The sick boy couldn't go wandering around. The only treatment that seemed to be helpful, other than the antibody, was rest. He might kill himself moving about in his condition.

This was one of the few times when there was no one to be seen on the street, of course. Bob muttered in disgust and went running toward the hospital. He should find his father there, and perhaps Kirby. He dashed past most of the houses.

Then he was in front of the laboratory that had been fixed up for his father.

It was only a vague hunch. He had no real reason to expect to find Red there. But it had been the chief center of his work since the return to the colony, and a man in delirium might decide to go where he had spent so much of his time.

Bob swung in. The airlock seemed to stick, but he got through it, blinking in the dim light inside. There was only one bulb burning.

Under it, Red sat at one of the tables, with Penny beside him. There was a maze of equipment near him, and the little bottle of plasma was in front of him. He looked up at the sound of Bob's entrance and reached for the bottle.

"Get back, Bob," he said. "I know what I'm doing. And if you try to stop me or go for help, I'll break this to smithereens! Uncle Frank wouldn't take any more blood from you, either."

"You can't do it," Bob protested.

"I can and will. You told me this was mine. What I do with it is my own business. And don't think you can appeal to Penny. We talked this over and we're working as a team."

The girl looked serious and a little scared, but she nodded violent agreement.

Bob wasn't sure whether Red was delirious or not. The words were clear and there was no wildness to him. He seemed colder and more sure of himself than usual. But that could be a form of delirium, too. And the boy's face was flushed with fever still.

Bob dropped to a seat, watching the other intently, but trying to act as if he'd given in. "All right, Red. But you might know you could trust me, if it's something important. What gives?"

"A debt that has to be paid, that's all. You should know about it. Penny says you are the one who finally managed to find out about the Jovians."

Bob could have choked the girl at the moment for talking so much! But maybe Red had managed to drag it out of her when she first evaded his natural question about what they had found. It didn't matter now.

"And I suppose you know what they need," he suggested.

Red nodded. "I figured it out. It should be obvious. They've got the same plague we have, and that's what's killing them. And they're looking for help in finding what it is and what will cure it."

"I see. Jovians have flesh exactly like ours and are subject to our diseases, eh? Well, I can't argue with you." Bob watched for any reaction. He was almost sure now that Red was delirious.

But Red didn't seem bothered by the question. He grinned tightly. "Don't pull that, Bob. You've heard your father explain often enough that there is evidence all life in the Solar System is like that on Earth—maybe even was spread from Earth spores. We don't know how it could have adapted to live on Jupiter, but we still can't figure out how it can exist on Titan, either. And you also heard your own father explain why the organism causing the plague can attack everything from a Gany plant to a human. Why can't it be dangerous to Jovians? Maybe not in the same way, but dangerous. They've been around here to pick it up after it mu-

168

tated. And Penny has shoved enough things into that globe to have let some of the plague in."

He had it worked out. And now Bob was less sure himself. The trouble was that the idea might have some logic in it. It would explain why the Jovians expected help from the humans here. If they knew that the men were sick, they might conclude that there was a way of treating things. He had no idea what information they might have picked up from Penny.

Red went on. "All right. They are entitled to whatever aid we can give. They helped us all they could, when they were too sick to have any right to operate their ship. If aliens can act like that, men have to return the debt."

"How, Red?"

"By giving them the best we have. A sample of the plague, so they can see what they are fighting, and some of the antibody, so they can figure out what will cure it for us. Maybe it won't work for them, but it will give them a hint, and that may be all they need. And maybe it won't work, but at least they'll die knowing we tried."

Bob nodded slowly. "I guess you're right," he admitted. "I don't think you're going at it the right way, but I guess we have to do what we can."

He saw Red relax a little for the first time. Then he launched himself in one long leap.

His hand found the bottle and caught it carefully. He had no time to try to fall gracefully. His suit hit the floor hard, and he went skidding on his face plate, but he had managed to keep the bottle from harm, even while his stomach churned from the shock of his landing.

He got to his feet, shoving the precious bottle through the little trap door into his suit. "All right, Red," he said. "We'll talk it over later. But right now, you're going back to your bed. And Penny, the next time you try to play conspirator, I won't wait for your father to take care of what ails you. Do you really want to kill Red? Because that's what you're doing. Get out of here and get your father!"

She got. He must have looked pretty horrible. His nose had struck the front of the helmet, and he was aware that a trickle of blood had smeared across his face plate. And he was angry enough to convince her. She darted out toward the entrance, screaming. He was pretty sure she would find McCarthy.

"I can crack my helmet open out there," Red threatened.

"I don't think you're that hysterical," Bob told him. "I think you've got a lot of adrenalin and other things in your system right now that are somehow keeping you rational, but still not as much yourself as you should be. I'll take the samples up to the Jovians."

Red stared up at him doubtfully, and then some of the forced strength seemed to drain out of him. He must have been operating on the thin edge of hysteria in order to keep going at all. "You mean it?"

"I mean it. I'm the logical choice for this job, Red. I can come a lot closer to finding some code to let them know what we're giving them than you can. That's my specialty, remember. And I'm just as concerned about our ethical obligations to those creatures out there as you are. Come on, let's get you home before you really collapse."

Red shook as he tried to get out of his sitting position. He was beginning to let the iron control go, and reaction was hitting him. But he still held some discipline over himself.

With Bob's arm around him, he managed to reach the entrance, and they began moving down the street. Then McCarthy was beside them, with a now thoroughly frightened Penny trotting behind him. Together, Bob and McCarthy got Red into the house, out of his suit, and into the bed.

Bob drew out the bottle of plasma, and Red started to get up again. "I won't take it!"

"Quiet down," McCarthy suggested evenly. "Why won't you take it?"

He listened as Bob told him the basic facts. Surprisingly, he seemed to accept the idea. "I don't know," he admitted. "But I guess you have to try. Red, there's enough plasma here for you *and* for a sample. You don't need much more than half of this. Now, stick out your arm."

He gave the injection and stood watching. The last fight was going out of Red now. Mrs. McCarthy came in, and the doctor turned the boy over to her. Penny was nowhere in sight. She knew enough not to bring any more fury on herself.

McCarthy put an arm over Bob's shoulder as they climbed the stairs. "I owe you a lot," he said. "But I guess there isn't much to say."

"I still don't know how delirious Red was," Bob said. He felt warm and pleased, but somewhat embarrassed by the doctor's praise.

McCarthy shrugged. "He wasn't exactly delirious, but he wasn't very rational either, I suspect. Sometimes a fever

171

can make a man's mind work like an electric motor with too high a voltage. It goes fast, but it isn't normal. Are you going up to the globe? If you are, I'll have Dan drive you up in the tractor."

He headed back for the hospital, and Bob turned to the laboratory. There he began looking over the preparations Red had made. They were puzzling. Apparently Red had been almost too logical in his guessing about the possible trouble with the Jovians, but he'd been hazy and confused about how to execute his plan.

Bob was about to go for his father when Dr. Wilson came in. It was obvious that McCarthy had briefed him already, but he asked a number of questions that Bob had to answer in detail. They were the penetrating questions of a trained scientist faced with a critical problem, and they were ones that could be answered exactly. In the end, he seemed as well informed as Bob was.

"I think it's a wild chance," he said as he began going through the slides and specimens. "Red left out a large number of doubtful factors, and he glossed over a lot of others. But there is a small chance he might be right, from what you tell me. And I can't argue with his ethics. Those creatures tried to make a bargain—and a good one for both sides. When it failed, they went through with their part of it anyhow. Now it's up to us to keep our part if we can. I guess the obligation is even greater than it would have been if we'd promised them help before they delivered the capsule."

He began to explain to Bob the various slides. He had chosen normal microscope slides, since there was no way of knowing that the creatures would have anything like an electron microscope. And he had picked out nothing which could not stand being subjected to the high pressure and weird atmosphere that might be found inside a ship from Jupiter.

"I'll fractionate this plasma and desiccate the antibody that is useful," he said. "Then we can put that into a plastic seal that will protect it. The rest is up to you."

16 / Decision

HOW DOES A MAN communicate with an alien? It was one of the oldest questions of the space age, but no man had ever been forced to decide on the answer before. There were theories. Elaborate systems had been worked out. There was even a handbook that had been prepared fifty years before Bob was born. In it, a series of mathematical symbols and pictures were evolved step by step to make certain that there could be no error in the interpretation.

The only trouble was that it hadn't worked. Bob remembered that someone had finally decided to try it out on a normal human who spoke a different language. An anthropologist had taken it to one of the few isolated areas where the technical revolution had not made a common culture necessary. And there a man who was well educated in his own language, and who had a high intelligence, had spent nearly a month poring over the book. In the end, it had not been possible to carry on an intelligent conversation beyond what simple signs would have provided.

And nearly all of those ideas were based on the assumption that one stone was one stone in every culture. But suppose there was a race that did not have a word for *one* or for *stone?* Suppose the unit one was only a spot on a line connecting something less than one with something more? On Earth, calculus already treated one in such a manner. And suppose a stone could be considered a relation between a hungry man and a rabbit, or a part of a long process that connected silt with pressure with cliffs with erosion? Either was valid. And neither was exclusive.

But to describe a stone was certainly simpler than to try to compress all that science had learned about disease and immunology into a few simple notes for a race that might have an entirely different way of looking at even the basic parts of science.

Bob had no time for long theorizing. And his mind had already skimmed over almost everything in his studies of analytic linguistics. He had only the very basic approach to thought that such a study could produce—the only vital part of science.

"You'd better sterilize everything, Dad," he called out. "We don't want to give them other troubles."

"Already thought of that. We'll pack everything into a sterile bag, and you can pour it out of that without touching anything again," Dr. Wilson assured him.

The problem of numbers came first. He chose a line to represent one, a square for two. Those could be drawn. But beyond that, he could not be sure. In the end, he rejected the whole scheme. He had to get along even without numbers, except as relationships.

A curve was his final solution. He went back to a curve for a simple tone—a sine wave—for one. Then one with a single overtone would stand for two. A third harmonic changed that and gave him three. He needed only five numbers to show the order of his slides, and a curve with even the fifth harmonic could be drawn. He used the symbol they had already agreed meant death for the dangerous organism. For the antibody, a series of waves died away toward the center but then grew larger again, to indicate recovery.

It took longer than he liked, but in the end, he had everything he needed based on curves. There were basic laws of physics involved in those—the whole mathematics of curves had been an almost necessary development to express such laws, and any race should be able to decode them, particularly one where curves were a normal code.

He encoded the slides carefully in their proper order, trying to simplify even the basic procedure that his father suggested. In the end, he was far from satisfied, but Dr. Wilson was impressed.

"I never thought much of this idea of science in language," he admitted. "But now I don't know. Maybe you're right, Bob. Maybe we don't have any idea yet of how to develop and handle our symbols. You've compressed your information a lot more than I thought possible. Certainly I can follow your instructions."

Bob hoped another form of life could do as well.

He had thought of taking Penny, but finally decided against it. If he couldn't arouse the globe, it seemed doubtful that she could. The last time, they had turned to him. Apparently, they were . . . fond? Something like that . . . At least they seemed to like her. But they needed a more mature mind and code now.

176

17 / The Long Wait

THE LIFT IN SPIRITS that had come from the return of the capsule and the efforts to repay the debt began to fade during the next three days. There was no more encouragement. From Earth came the report of more difficulty in making the antibody than had been expected. It now seemed that there would be no chance of getting even a pilot batch of it for at least a month, and then there would be still the long trip for another capsule.

The cases of sickness continued to increase. The number had now reached nearly a hundred. The patients were jammed into the hospital, and another building was being converted to handle those who were now being treated at home. In another week or so, if the increase continued, half the colony might be sick. After that, the only question was whether there would be enough who could somehow escape or recover to care for the new cases.

Mars got in touch with them that day. Nobody had thought of appealing to that planet, since there were supposed to be no independent spaceships outside of the control of Earth. But the colonials had found an old ship that had been scrapped, and they had managed to recondition it. Now it was in space, heading toward Ganymede at the maximum acceleration it could make, and there were doctors and nurses among the volunteers. Mars, it seemed, had a long memory, and her own plague was still not forgotten.

It would take more than three months before the aged rockets could bring that help, of course. But the people in Outpost didn't have to be told that. It was a pitiful effort, but at least there was another world that was trying.

"The old *Alabama*," Kirby said when the message came through. "I never shipped on her, but she was a cantankerous tub from the day they built her. Been rusting for sixty years now. I wonder where they found officers and crew to take her out to space." Then he grinned. "But I'll bet she makes it!"

It seemed probable. She'd already managed to stand the high thrust of her initial acceleration off Mars, and she would be coasting from there until she neared Ganymede.

Kirby nodded. "Reminds me of the time when Davy Dreadnaught ran out of fuel coming back from Neptune. Dunno how he did it, but there he was, halfway back, and no fuel for his rockets. So he put his boys out with nets. Sure enough, just as he thought, along came a comet a-streaking toward the Sun. It was a big one, and Davy finally had to go out with his own net to catch it. But he got it, and he stuffed it into his fuel tanks. The comet tail went a-rushing out the rocket tubes. Gave him a steady two gees of acceleration all the way back. He beat the all-time record."

Bob considered it, realizing that this was supposed to be one where Davy hadn't made a mistake. Then he spotted the trouble, and grinned. "All right, Dan. If the comet tail was blasting all the way, how did he decelerate to land on Earth? Or did he crash?"

Kirby chuckled. "I'm surprised at you, Bob. The Earth was on the other side of the sun. Everybody knows a comet's tail points away from the sun. So when Davy got opposite that, the tail whipped the ship around and began decelerating all the way back to Earth."

They sobered almost at once, though. There was nothing humorous on Ganymede now. Yet Bob had begun to feel respect for the people here again. They had gone through their low ebb and were now taking the threat of the plague with fear, but also with courage. They were fighting, not crying, over their bad luck. There was little they could do, but they were trying.

Red was mending slowly, but he was still unconscious most of the time. He probably should have had a second shot of the antibody, but there was no more available now. Most of the others had to get by without even that, Bob realized, but he still wished McCarthy had been willing to accept his offer to donate more for Red.

"He'll get well," Kirby decided as they sat down at the dinner table. "He's gotta. And then he can look forward to a mighty long life. Even this cursed plague has some blessings."

Wilson confirmed what Kirby had said. "You're probably right, Dan. I've been running some tests in my free time, and the plague does seem to produce strange side effects. One is a stimulation of certain cells that seem to govern the body's ability to rejuvenate itself. If this could be controlled, it would probably give the whole human race enough time

181

to make better use of life—at least an average age beyond a hundred."

Bob wasn't too greatly interested in that, though. At present he was more worried about Red's ability to survive the next few days than his own chance of living for a hundred years.

Then it was his turn to take a shift at the hospital. Much as he hated the work, he had volunteered for it. He went in with butterflies in his stomach and came out later in a state of both physical and mental exhaustion, but he couldn't do less now.

Two more slow days crept by, with the sick toll mounting steadily. It seemed impossible that there had been less than twenty deaths so far, but that couldn't last. Many of the patients were reaching a state where their hearts couldn't take much more.

Red was just beginning to get better when Penny came down with the plague. Like Red's, it seemed to be a mild case at first, but McCarthy was sick with worry. The disease seemed to be harder on the young than on older people. Mrs. McCarthy nearly collapsed, but then she gathered her inner strength and went on firmly. She was a woman of much more strength than most people would have guessed from her usual manner.

A few people seemed able to recover from the disease by themselves, and Bob had expected that these might yield enough antibodies to save many more. But even that hope failed. They were willing to contribute their blood, but the yield of the precious saving molecules was much lower than had been true for Bob's blood. He remembered that McCarthy had commented on his phenomenal production of the antibodies, and it seemed to be true. His body was one of those that seemed most capable of putting up a strong fight against any infection.

But there was one other on Ganymede who did better at that than he could, as he learned by accident. Dr. Wilson had deliberately infected himself right after Bob's recovery. In his case, the disease had been no more than a mild headache and light fever that nobody else had noticed. But it had produced the antibodies in large quantities. It had resulted in the saving of a few lives already, but McCarthy now refused to take more blood from him. And those saved by the use of antibodies from others seemed to develop less of their own, so that they were of little help.

Earth reported that the trouble with the process had been solved by a group of biochemists and that the operation of the pilot plant had begun. They were promising now that they could put the first batch on the rocket within the three-week period they had first named. It was supposed to be encouraging news, but nobody on Ganymede bothered to comment on it. By the time the serum could arrive, the only ones alive would be those who had already recovered.

It was the fifth day after Bob had visited the globe that it appeared again. There was a bustle at the hospital entrance, during Bob's duty shift, and someone came running toward him, urging him to go out. He tumbled into his suit and went onto the street. There, most of the people who were still not infected were looking up.

The globe was circling overhead slowly, and there was no uncertainty this time. It moved smoothly, obviously wanting those below to know that it was moving again. Then at last it lifted upward and disappeared in a rush toward Jupiter.

People cheered and waved, as if it had been a rescue rocket for themselves. But the cheering was brief as they went back to their own worries.

Bob felt a lift of relief, too. There was the satisfaction of having somehow managed to do the job correctly, and the very genuine pleasure of knowing that at least some on board the globe had lived. The human race had managed to pay its debt to another race.

Penny was in a raging fever at the time she heard the news, but she seemed to understand. She smiled weakly, and her parched lips moved in a whisper. "Nice—they were awful nice people."

Red was also pleased, as he had a right to be, since he had now been proved right. He was beginning to get better finally, and the news seemed to help.

But Bob realized that the departure of the ship was also the end of what might have been their only hope. If he could have known in time to reach the ship again, and if he could have found some way to communicate, he would have made another appeal to the Jovians.

Their ship was much faster than even the *Procyon*. With it, they could have reached Earth in time to pick up the capsule that would be sent out with the antibodies. Then there might have been a chance for the serum to save at least a few hundred of the men who were almost certainly going to die.

Now there was only the long wait until the disease ran its course.

The next day, the doctor came down with the plague.

18 / New Frontiers

SOMETIMES NOW IT SEEMED to Bob that all of Outpost was one huge hospital ward. He finished his shift in the old building and moved wearily toward the second one, where Dr. McCarthy was raging deliriously. The man was undergoing one of the worst cases Bob had seen. The long, driving hours and the strain of the past weeks must have worn him down to the point of collapse before the disease hit. And probably he had also managed to go on for a time, even after it began to attack him.

They were turning another building into a hospital as he moved up the street, and there should have been still more room. He stopped to wait for Kirby, who was supervising the alterations. The old man came out, walking slowly. He was driving himself beyond even his limits, and he was nearing the end of his strength. But he lifted a hand and grinned.

Bob tried to smile back, but he found it hard. The question came into his mind, as it must always occur whenever two people met now: How long before he comes down with the plague?

Sanchez came out a few minutes later. His dark face was

wet with sweat inside his helmet. "Be ready tomorrow," he decided as he looked back at the third hospital building. "Dunno what building we can use for the next one."

He seemed to take it for granted that there would be another. But Bob wondered. How much longer could those who were well go on carrying the load?

They stood there in the street, too tired to go to the meals that were waiting for them in the community kitchen. The few women left, who were not full-time nurses, could not prepare separate meals. Everyone ate together now, to save work.

Luis Sanchez lifted his head with a flick to knock a drop of perspiration away from his eye. His head stayed back, and his jaw slowly opened. One hand raised upward.

Bob followed the pointing finger.

From the north, a globe had appeared. Then a second came into view, to be followed by a third. The two rear ones were smaller than the first but otherwise the same. And the front one looked like the one he had seen before, while the other two were a dull grey. But they all flew with the same smooth grace, and all were heading straight for Outpost.

For a second, they hovered together in the air. Then they spread out, finding places to land.

One of the dull ones touched first. Almost at once, a small door opened in its side and objects began spilling out. They looked like little plastic cubes.

Bob grabbed up one, staring at it. It was similar to the container Dr. Wilson had made for the dried antibody serum, but much larger. It seemed to contain about an ounce of some powder. And on the outside, in clear white, was an inscribed series of curves. They were the same curves Bob had used to indicate the antibody in the sample he had placed in the Jovian ship.

He looked at the pile before him and at an equal pile that was spilling from a door in the second small ship. As he looked, the doors closed, and the two dull ships lifted, leaving only the larger, brighter one and the two piles of containers.

There were enough of the containers in either pile to give every man, woman, and child on Ganymede at least a dozen apiece.

He let out a shout, calling for attention. The people turned toward him slowly, uncertain as to what this all meant. But Sanchez had already decided what the piles contained. The mayor raised one in each hand, waving them toward the gathering crowd.

"The antibody!" His voice was almost musical as he cried it. "We got the antibody now, folks. Our friends from Jupiter have come back to save us!"

Wilson came up, shaking his head mildly as he heard the words. "It might have been better to find out first before you start getting peoples' hopes up," he warned. But his own face was breaking into a smile as he saw the symbols inscribed on the container. He grabbed a handful of the packages and motioned to Bob. "Come on, let's test this!"

They began dissolving the powder from a few capsules in distilled water, even before he could start his tests. Sanchez was already going to find the nurses who had been trained to give injections and to locate every hypodermic in the colony.

Dr. Wilson made a quick check in the optical microscope. "Seems sterile, at least," he said. He made a longer inspection in the electron microscope and then hovered over some of the disease culture that had received a drop of the serum.

"We might as well try it," he decided. "It looks and acts like the antibody. It would take three days to be absolutely sure it is identical, anyway. Either we trust our new friends or we don't."

Nobody argued or suggested caution. The three nurses with the hypodermics began moving through the hospitals, giving a massive dose to everyone. There was more serum now than could ever be used. And among the first to get treatments were Dr. McCarthy and Penny.

Bob wandered out at last, to see the globe still waiting in the middle of Outpost. He headed for it, wondering how one could say thanks in symbolic mathematics. He had to try, though, even though the fatigue in his legs seemed about to make him collapse with every step.

He was yawning as he went up to the ship and reached for the panel. But the screen above had lighted before he could touch the ship. There was a distorted picture of Penny there, also yawning, and then another of her curled up as if sleeping. They were clearer than most of the Jovian pictures. Then another flashed on, so distorted that it took him nearly a minute to guess that it was supposed to represent his face as it had been when he yawned.

The two lines appeared, blended into one, and then shortened into a dot before vanishing. "Good-by!"

The ship took off, cruising slowly toward the north. It

began dropping toward the Bowl as he watched, as if settling down to wait for him.

It was three days later before the last of the patients treated with the serum was able to get up and move around, but recovery had been rapid under the doses made possible by the present from Jupiter. There had been no more deaths, and now the hospitals were being emptied of their cots and reconverted to their original uses.

In three days, it seemed, people could get used to almost anything. Only a few were clustered around Bob and Penny as they sat before the great Jovian globe, taking turns at trying to communicate. Most of the others were willing to wait until later when they could all meet and find out what he had learned, if they liked.

This time, when the globe signed off and lifted into space it moved upward, heading back toward Jupiter. But by now they had established enough of a crude mixture of signs and pictures for it to explain that it would be back in another week for more mutual study.

Bob watched it go, smiling a little. Men had needed an alien language to compare with their own and to find how to build an even better one that both men and machines could use. He'd been ready to spend his life trying to create such a non-human speech once. And now, on a little outpost world, the language had come to him, more alien than he had dreamed possible.

He'd probably never learn to think in it, but Penny had gone a long ways toward that goal with what he called the "baby sign language" of the two lines the Jovians had simplified for her. He would have to open the ways to understanding, but she would attain it.

He already knew enough of the story of the ship to report to the people here. The guess Red had made had been close enough to the truth, and the antibody had reached the sick Jovians almost too late. But in some unexplainable way they had managed to give their remaining strength to one of their group who had then been able to discover the cure from a study of Bob's notes and samples. They couldn't use the same serum, of course, but they found one that acted the same. After that, they had headed back to Jupiter, where human serum could be made and where a great dance—or what seemed to be a dance—had been celebrated all over their world at their joy in having found that humans could become friends.

Penny had gone off to join Red and Dr. McCarthy inside the house, where Mrs. McCarthy would be cooking twice as much as they all could eat.

Bob walked down the street more slowly, nodding to his friends. Sanchez called out, but the mayor was in too much of a hurry to stop. He was trying to get ready for what he felt would be an unlimited and ever brighter future, with Outpost as the trading center for the two cultures, and the plague from the dumbspike as an eternal source of riches. Now that it could be controlled by the serum, there should be customers for it as long as men wanted to live to a great age without the handicaps of senility. Bob smiled after the mayor. Maybe the future still had troubles, but it also had a lot of promise for Ganymede.

He stopped at the laboratory to call his father to dinner, but he knew it was useless. Dr. Wilson looked up from the few tiny samples of Jovian plant life the ship had been able to find on board and pass out; he was more interested in that than in food.

For a moment, Bob paused outside the house, waiting for Kirby as the old man came up the street.

Kirby nodded toward the colony. "Looks good. I reckon they don't need me any more, so I'm going back to my farm tomorrow." He squinted thoughtfully up toward the black sky that never changed. "Looks like good weather for weeding is about due. You doing anything special tomorrow?"

Bob shook his head. "Not a thing, Dan." There really wasn't anything much for him to do. The ship would be gone for a week, and Sanchez had already assigned the clerical work to his daughter, Maria. He suddenly realized that there literally wasn't a thing for him to do.

"Good." Kirby grinned slowly. "Then you come out. Maybe I'll make a decent farmer out of you yet."

Bob threw one arm over the old man's shoulder and turned into the house with him. "I'd like that fine," he said.

He meant it.

About the Author

LESTER DEL REY is no stranger to readers of science fiction and science fact. Several of his books have received special notice; *Marooned on Mars* received a Boy's Club of America Award, and *Rockets Through Space* won the Thomas Alva Edison Award for the best science book in the children's book field in 1960. It was praised by scientists as demonstrating a keen understanding of the problems involved in space travel.

A long series of occupations preceded Mr. del Rey's highly successful writing career. After graduating from George Washington University in Washington, D.C., he worked at various times as a carpenter, hotel clerk, farmer, photographer, and advertising man. His interests cover as wide a range as his occupations have—from philology, linguistics, and history to cooking, cabinet-making, and the repairing of old typewriters, which he buys for that express purpose.

Kirby was waiting in the tractor, and Sanchez had decided to drive it. The mayor had already taken on a personal responsibility for the aliens, it seemed.

Bob tried to explain what he was hoping to accomplish. He was not surprised when both men seemed doubtful of his attempt to communicate. But it didn't matter. They were agreed on the one important thing—that men had to give the help that had been asked if there was any way to give it.

The tractor reached the top of the Bowl and began threading downward. In a minute, Bob could see the globe below. There was no change in it, and the little trailer stood there with its pitiful offerings still waiting. There was no evidence of life or activity, and the outside of the globe was free of any signs.

Bob had hoped that there might be some response before he had to approach the ship. But there was none. He moved over to the panel on which he had communicated previously.

Now his doubts were greater than ever. But it was too late to change his plans. He reached forward and made a dot. Then he moved his finger outward to form a straight line. And finally, he executed the other three sides of a square. From no dimension, one; from one dimension, two—and a pattern. He had told them previously that there was no dimension or extension to his ability—now he was trying to show that that had been increased or extended.

But there was no answer. He waited for a while and tried it again. And again everything remained blank on the big panel above. For all he knew, he was too late, and they might all be dead. But as long as he could lift his arm, he meant to keep trying.

He had made the fifth try before there was any response. Then it was only the opening of the little door. The big panel still held no signal.

He moved forward and carefully dumped the contents of the little plastic bag into the tunnel the door revealed.

A minute later the door closed.

There was no other sign of life, but he had done all he could now. He climbed back into the tractor and signaled for Sanchez to drive away.

When he looked back before they rounded the bend in the trial, the great globe was unchanged.

If the help was not enough or if it had come too late, the globe might stand there forever, he realized. And nobody would ever know whether the fault was his or not.